"Have you been sniffing the paste stick again?"

I could not believe that Lindsay DeWitt was sitting in my cubicle, asking me to be her date to her mother's wedding. There had to be a punch line—probably with an actual punch. But she looked totally serious, a little miserable, and sort of cute.

"Why don't you ask Biff or Skip or Chipwich or any of those other blue bloods who have pictures of the Mayflower in their living rooms?" I said. "Why me?"

Lindsay stared at her shoes like they might talk for her. "I sort of told my family you were already my date, Daniel."

She leveled those deep brown eyes at me. Something inside me felt a little electric jolt, and I had this urge to make everything better for her. I don't know why.

"I couldn't help it," she said. "Everyone was going on about the wedding and dates, and they all looked at me like I was a dateless dork and . . . and besides, it'll just be the same dumb guys from the same families there, and I don't even want my mom to get married again, and . . . and I don't know what I'm saying. Just forget I asked, okay?"

Yeah, right.

Love Stories

His. Hers. Theirs.

The Nine-hour Date

EMMA HENRY

BANTAM BOOKS

NEW YORK · TORONTO · LONDON · SYDNEY · AUCKLAND

RL: 6, AGES 012 AND UP

THE NINE-HOUR DATE
A Bantam Book / February 2001

Cover photography by Barry Marcus.

Produced by 17th Street Productions,
an Alloy Online, Inc. company.
33 West 17th Street
New York, NY 10011.

ISBN: 0-553-49370-1

Visit us on the Web! www.randomhouse.com/teens

Published simultaneously in the United States and Canada

Bantam Books is an imprint of Random House Children's Books, a
division of Random House, Inc. BANTAM BOOKS and the rooster
colophon are registered trademarks of Random House, Inc. Bantam Books,
1540 Broadway, New York, New York 10036.

PRINTED IN THE UNITED STATES OF AMERICA

OPM   0 9 8 7 6 5 4 3 2 1

One

Lindsay

I COULDN'T EXPLAIN how a sixteen-year-old girl who'd only been on two parent-arranged dates ended up writing an advice column called "A Girl's/Guy's View" for an online girls' magazine called *Blink*. It probably had something to do with high-school interns and slave labor being used in the same sentence a lot. Anyway, it was a great summer internship (three days a week) for a budding writer. I was hunkered down in my cubicle when my mentor (and *Blink* senior editor), Ann, stopped by.

"Working on a toughie?" asked Ann.

"Yep," I said. "Desperate in Des Moines wants to know if she should take her boyfriend back. He broke up with her right before Valentine's Day in order to avoid the whole flowers-gift scene."

"I see," said Ann. "What's your verdict?"

"I say dump him. If he can't handle a few roses for Valentine's Day, it doesn't bode well for prom."

Ann tilted her head. "Maybe he can't afford roses and was too embarrassed to admit it. Did you consider what might lie behind his decision?"

"He could've at least gotten her a card," I countered. I had to admit, I was pretty much in righteous-girl mode when I'd made my decision.

"Maybe you could run it by Daniel. Get his feel for it."

At the name of Daniel Newman, all thoughts of charity disappeared. "He'll say that Valentine's Day was thought up by girls to force boys to take them out where all their friends could see them." I hadn't meant to sound like a fourth grader having a pity party, but any mention of Daniel made me mental. He was my high-school counterpart for the advice column—the guy of "A Girl's/Guy's View." We rarely offered the same advice, which was why our column was so popular. Daniel Newman and I couldn't agree on which way to pet a cat.

Ann laughed. "He is original."

"What he is is *obnoxious,*" I blurted out without thinking. I peered up at Ann to see if I was in trouble, but she was holding back a smile.

Okay. Honest-revelation time? Daniel was way cute, in a disheveled, maniac-in-training sort of way. He had short, scruffy blond hair with an attempt at musician sideburns. Huge, swimming pool blue eyes surrounded by foot-long lashes. If I saw him on the street, I'd definitely look twice and wonder where he kept his bass guitar and old VW Bug. But when Daniel opened his mouth, it was good-bye, fantasy boy, hello, lord–God–king–of–my own–domain attitude. We'd been working together for four weeks and got along like rats and laboratories, plaids and stripes.

"Almost forgot why I dropped by," Ann said. "We're meeting in the conference room for a quickie status in three."

I grabbed a notebook and my favorite black pen and followed Ann down the long hallway to the *Blink* conference room.

Jenny Jenson took the seat next to me. She had just graduated from the Fashion Institute of Technology, where I was sure she had majored in style. She was a poster child for cool in her gray capris and Moschino shirt. I was still wearing the same J. Crew khakis and pastel sweater sets I'd worn since sixth grade.

"Hey, Lindsay," Jenny said. "You heard it here first. I'm predicting pink will be very big this fall. It's going to be the new black."

"What's wrong with the old black?" I shrugged.

"It's so tired. Here, look," she said, showing me a layout from the September issue. That was the weirdest thing about magazine life. Working three or four months ahead always made me a little dizzy.

"How much?" I asked, looking at a pair of impossibly high heels that would make my size-nine boat feet look even more ship ahoy.

"Three hundred and fifteen dollars," Jenny said wistfully. "I'd have to sell a kidney to wear them. It might almost be worth it."

"Call me wacky, but I'm thinking shoes are not worth a major organ."

"Easy for you to say. You're loaded."

I cringed. I was hoping the start of my journalism career would mean the end of my job as professional rich girl. "We're not that rich, Jenny," I said. It was so not true. My family was that rich and then some.

Jenny actually snorted. "Yeah, right. Everybody lives with three maids, a cook, a landscaper, and a famous mom. Oh, speaking of . . ." Jenny handed me three phone messages from our ditzy receptionist. The one who could never remember where I sit. The messages all said *Call your mom*.

My mom. Now, there was a woman who could use an around-the-clock advice columnist. Maybe you've heard of her? Caroline DeWitt. That's the short version. The long version is Caroline Langenkamp DeWitt Chapman Yellowfeather Smith. In the gossip pages it was usually "socialite-turned-TV-reporter" Caroline DeWitt. My mom had been married so many times that Bergdorf's had a revolving door in their china department just for her. Okay, I'm kidding about the door. But my mom had never had a great track record when it came to marriage.

Husband number one had been Charles DeWitt, aka Dad. They'd been young. Beautiful. Totally in love. Also filthy rich. My mom grew up on yachts and in ballrooms. My dad was from old money in England, plus he had that yummy accent that made a phrase like "where's the bathroom?" sound like the intro to a show on PBS. Together they were like the Barbie and Ken of New York society. My mom wore a lot of new clothes. My dad played a lot of polo. And then I came along. I don't think they were quite ready for that because two years later my dad was off to Europe, where he spent most of his time, and my mom and I moved into an apartment on Fifth Avenue with the much talked about servants and gardeners. My dad sent a lot of postcards from far-off places. It was supposed to make me feel like I was almost there. Funny thing was, it only made me feel impossibly far away.

I was just wondering what sale my mom had to tell me about that had inspired her to call *Blink* three times when Daniel Newman raced in, all irritated. "I don't really have time for a meeting," he said, plunking down in the seat next to Jenny. He was wearing his Eat the Rich T-shirt and old jeans. He hadn't shaved in a few days, and it looked really amazing on him. Not that I would ever tell him that.

"So, Lindsay," Jenny said, leaning in close to me. "What's the dish? Is your mom still dating Jeffrey Forrester?"

"They've been dating," I told her, "but it's nothing serious." I wasn't sure if I was telling the truth or just reassuring myself.

"He is so dreamy!" Jenny whispered. "And he's only, like, one of the richest men in the world. He owns half of cable television plus the South Carolina Tigers."

"Yeah, I guess." The conversation was starting to make me itch.

"Omigod!" Jenny exclaimed. "That reminds me! *Vogue* just did a whole layout on Alison Forrester. Here, look." Jenny flipped through the pages till she found one of a flawless teenage blonde stepping out of a limo. The headline read, *A Day in the Life of a Teen Queen*. There was Alison in all her fashion-plate glory. A picture of Alison at a gala ball for Debs Who Care. A picture of Alison talking on her cell phone while having lunch at some trendy café. A picture of Alison with her field-hockey team at her Connecticut boarding school. She was the only one not covered in mud. And a picture of Alison arm in arm with her famous model/actor boyfriend, Marlon Cassidy. An article on me would need only two pictures: me sitting at a computer at *Blink* or me reading a book in my bedroom on Fifth Avenue. No boys. No cafés. No hairdo tips (unless the ponytail counted).

"Ooh, Alison Forrester," Daniel said, looking over Jen's shoulder. "Just what we need—more pages of blond girls shopping." For once Daniel and I were in agreement.

Jenny ignored him. "So have you ever, like, hung out with Alison? Now that your mom and her dad are dating and all?"

My mom was dating Alison Forrester's dad. I

had never thought about it that way before. In fact, I'd tried not to think about it at all. This put everything in a whole new light. An ugly, beyond fluorescent light. "Nope," I said, uncapping my pen and pretending to get prepared for our quickie meeting. "Never have, never will."

"But your mom and her dad . . ."

"Look, Jen, my mom and Jeffrey Forrester will probably be history by next weekend. She's dated a new guy every other month for the past three years." I didn't mean to sound so irritated, but I couldn't face the thought of that dippy Alison Forrester and me having anything in common. I'd seen her at a couple of parties here and there, and she gave rich girls a bad name. Fortunately Ann breezed in and interrupted the Jen-alogue.

"Hey, gang, this is just a quickie meeting for status and to do a little brainstorming on possible story ideas." Ann went around the table, asking everyone how their various projects were coming along. Then she opened the floor to new ideas. As usual, Daniel jumped right in.

"Um, Ann? I've been thinking we should do a hard-hitting exposé on sweatshops. You know, a lot of the places that manufacture some of America's most popular brands of clothing hire child labor and make them work fourteen-hour days for practically nothing—"

Jen butted in. "Sweatshops? But that's so icky. What about the new fall colors?"

Daniel looked at Jen like she had two heads and

blurted out, "Sure. Fall colors. Sweatshop labor. They're one and the same."

"All right, settle down," said Ann.

"Sorry, Jen," Daniel was decent enough to say, but Jen's attention was taken by a pair of leather pants in the *Vogue* she was flipping through for inspiration.

"I have an idea," I said, seizing the moment. "What about the debutante-ball scene? We could follow some girls as they get ready to make their debuts into society."

"I like it," Ann said with a smile. I was glad I hadn't sounded totally stupid. I really wanted Ann to like me. To think I was smart instead of just Lindsay DeWitt, privileged girl.

"You're kidding, right?" It was Daniel. "Who cares that a bunch of snobby cream puffs in white dresses get to do the big curtsy every year?"

"Excuse me, Mr. Champion of the Grunge Rock Nation, but some of us do care," I said, trying to sound extremely grown up.

"Well, of course you would. *DeWitt*."

I didn't like the way he said my name, like it had an oily film all over it. But before I could launch into a scathing diatribe, Ann's assistant burst into the room.

"Quick, turn on Channel 11. Lindsay's mom is making an announcement."

Ann grabbed the remote, and a full-color image of my mom crackled to life on the TV screen. She was wearing a beige silk suit. Her blond hair looked

8

even more radiant on camera. Watching her, I understood why men lined up to marry her.

I heard my mom's voice fill the room. ". . . now that the *Post* is about to leak the news, I feel that I should let the world know for sure, exclusively here on Channel 11, that yes, Jeffrey Forrester and I are engaged." The camera zoomed in on her left hand. She was wearing a brand-new rock the size of a small lapdog. "We plan to be married next month in a very special ceremony. That's all I'm saying for now. We'll give you more details as we figure them out." My mom smiled. She had one of the ten best smiles in New York, according to a poll of Manhattan dentists.

"Turn it off," I found myself saying quietly. The call-mom phone messages glared up at me in blue and white from their perch on my notebook. I was so mortified, I couldn't even look up from them and face the room—especially Daniel, who would be loving the whole thing. Mom was getting married, and she hadn't even told me first. A flush crept up from my stomach to my temples.

Unfortunately Jenny couldn't let me die a thousand deaths in peace. "Oh my God, you know what this means, don't you?" she screeched.

That my mom was rushing into another ill-fated, media-hyped marriage? That I could feel sorry for myself and take to my bed? That I needed to seek out some advice for myself for a change?

Jen leaned in for the kill. "Congratulations! You and Alison Forrester are about to be sisters!"

9

Daniel

Burn! It had to bite hard having your mom announce her wedding plans on TV. And to discover you were about to be joined under one roof with a total trendoid of a sister. It was almost too good to be true. The Debonator (combo of *debutante* and *terminator*) had just been handed a serious knock on her J. Crew–clad tush. I couldn't resist getting in one little dig. What I should have done was keep my big mouth shut.

"Hey, DeWitt, maybe *Blink* can do a profile of you and Alison becoming the big family unit. I'll bet our readers would be very interested in that," I said with my best earnest face. I was supposed to use my powers for good, not evil, but hey—I'm human.

Ann jumped on the story. "What an excellent idea, Mr. Newman. And you would be the perfect person to write that profile. Let's set a deadline, shall we?"

"I don't think that's such a good idea," Lindsay said. I knew I should be relieved, but I was a little insulted. Did she think I wasn't worthy of her life story? That I couldn't write? Still, I did not want to write this poufy girls' story.

"Yeah, I agree, Ann. I mean, I don't know anything about the bonding rituals of teenage girls. I might get hurt. And that would be irresponsible journalism."

Ann wasn't buying it. "Well, Daniel, journalists have to put themselves on the line every day. If you can't handle the Upper East Side, how are you going to cover a war zone someday?"

"But this is worse than war," I blurted out. "It's torture. It'll be an article filled with stuff about shoes and low-fat frozen yogurt and 'N Sync concerts."

"You'll survive," she answered.

Working at a girls' magazine was not my idea. In fact, as a career choice for a guy, I'd have to rate it right down there with handing out tuna snacks to tourists at Sea World. My dad was pretty torqued when I told him that I'd be spending my summer giving girls a guy's view of their love troubles and how to fix them. I dreaded giving him the news so much that I waited till dinner that night to tell him.

"You're kidding, right?" Robert Newman said over a traditional Newman dinner of frozen pizza and Cocoa Puffs right out of the box, no milk chaser.

When I shook my head, Dad said, "I see." Only my dad could make two little innocent words sound so full of disappointment. I seemed to disappoint my dad on a daily basis. It isn't like he's a bad guy or anything. He just has impossibly high standards. He's a lawyer for the ACLU (American Civil Liberties Union), so he's always looking out for the underdog. Believe it or not, he didn't count me in that category. When my mom was around, she used to be able to joke him out of it. She'd say something like, "Hey, Robert. I thought you were a defense lawyer, not a prosecutor. Take a break, okay?" And he'd smile in spite of himself. Since my mom died two years ago, he hadn't smiled at all. It was like she'd taken all his smiles with her.

After an uncomfortable pause, my dad started in again. "Why couldn't you intern at *Time* or *Newsweek*?"

"Yeah, you think they'd be bowled over the minute I announced my name in their offices, but believe it or not, they were unimpressed," I said sarcastically. My dad had a way of making me feel like a defensive five-year-old. (I had applied for every journalism internship imaginable. *Blink* was my only offer.)

Dad didn't flinch. Years in the courtroom had taught him how to control every facial muscle. "So where do you think this little summer stint will be taking you? Schools like Columbia and Stanford aren't terrible impressed by online girls' magazines, Daniel."

I was tempted to tell him that *Blink* was doing an article on Stanford wanting really sensitive men but decided to eat more Cocoa Puffs instead. "It's just temporary. Next summer I'm getting into *Newsweek* no matter what. Anyway," I said, making it up as I went along, "I'm trying to get them to do more hard-news stories, you know, stuff about sweatshops and all."

"Hmmm, good, Daniel. That's good. What are you working on now?"

I froze. I could not, absolutely not, tell my dad I was profiling Lindsay DeWitt and Alison Forrester. For one thing, my dad, the die-hard liberal, was majorly against rich people, and the Forresters and DeWitts made *Webster's* definition of rich. For another thing, it sounded so—don't hate me—girlie. "Oh," I said, hoping another mouthful of Puffs would distort what I was saying, "it's sort of a piece about these two families. You know, human-interest stuff. Whatever."

"Ummm," said my dad. "You'll have to let me read it." He eyed the clock. 7 P.M. "I'd better hit these files," he said, patting his briefcase. "Going out tonight?"

"I'm meeting Hakeem at The Coffeehouse in five minutes," I said. After telling me to be home at a decent hour, my dad disappeared into his bedroom, and I hit the streets. The Coffeehouse was only a few blocks away.

I found Hakeem in the crowded coffee lounge. He ordered us a couple of chai teas and overpriced muffins, and I swiped a table near the back, away from the stage in case the open mike (for poetry, writers, musicians, whatever) was a bust. I told him the DeWitt-Forrester dilemma.

"Ah, man, that's harsh," was Hakeem's take. "The Dan Man writing up stats on the deb crowd. This I gotta see."

It's a cruel world when even your best friend mocks your pain. "Dude, did I rip on you when you tried to grow dreads like Lenny Kravitz and

13

everybody called you mushroom head for two months?"

"Point taken," Hakeem said sheepishly.

"I mean, it's bad enough I have to write a column with Lindsay. Now I've gotta spend a whole day with her—and with Alison Forrester."

"You're going about this the wrong way, my man. Listen to what I'm saying: You, Daniel Newman, who hasn't had too much luck with your own type, get to spend the day with two very fine young ladies. *Capisce?*"

Okay, Alison was pretty much a dead ringer for Gwyneth Paltrow. But Lindsay? The Debonator? (*a*) She was *preppy*. And (*b*) she struck me as the type who'd never been in any situation she wasn't totally prepared for. Like she probably carried a small first-aid kit in her backpack just in case. I didn't get what Hakeem was after. "You think DeWitt is choice?"

Hakeem polished off his muffin and took a big gulp of a chai tea. "Yeah, she's choice. She's pretty, and I like the way she knows what she wants. It works for me. Hey, maybe I should go hang out with the Money Twins and watch them claw each other's eyes out while you sit around in your room, moping and listening to Eminem."

It hadn't dawned on me before, but of course Alison and Lindsay were bound to rub each other the wrong way. Maybe even get a little *Dawson's Creek* on me. Now, *that* was good stuff. "Whoa. Dude, that is brilliant. I can turn the profile into sort of an exposé. Wait for 'em to say or do something

14

embarrassing, then get it in print. I get to take Miss Smarty-pants down a notch and write a cool piece I won't be embarrassed about. He shoots! He scores! The crowd goes wild!" I put my hands up in the air in a mock cheer.

Hakeem rolled his eyes. "Dan-o. Always the reporter. Uh-oh. Looks like we're getting a folksinger next."

I looked over at the microphone area and saw a short, curvy chick in a Liz Phair T-shirt and old Levi's take the stage. She had dark, messy hair with a few blond streaks in it. She looked totally cool, waiflike, and a little dangerous—the anti-Lindsay. I instantly made it my mission in life to get her phone number.

"Hi. My name is Suki," she said in a soft voice.

Hakeem snickered. "I bet her name is really Betty Jo or Mary."

"I'd like to sing a song I wrote about a bad time in my life," Suki continued, "and this guy who broke up with me. It's called 'Pain Song.'" Suki kept her head down while she strummed her guitar. I made a mental note to go home and practice my own strumming later. I could see us traveling the back roads, hitting every open mike from New Jersey to California. It could happen.

Suki started singing, "'We used to be so close, you and me, you called me all the time. Then one day you said good-bye. Now all I do is cry. And everything is pain. Pizza, phone calls, and the rain. Everything is pain. Since you said good-bye.'"

I was totally in love. She sang two more songs. They were also about pain, but I kind of liked it as a theme. "Dude, I have met my perfect woman," I whispered to Hakeem. Suki was putting away her guitar.

I rushed to the stage and introduced myself and told her how much I liked her music. Then I went in for the kill. "Psycho Fish are coming to Irving Plaza next week. They've got this cool neo-punk-folk thing going on. Would you like to go with me?" You may not know this, but time actually expands in the moments between asking a girl out and having her answer. It was the slowest three seconds of my life.

Suki smiled—a good sign. "Wow. That sounds very real, Dabney."

"Daniel," I corrected.

"Uh, I'd love to go—"

"Cool," I interrupted. "I could pick you up at eight. We could get something to eat first and—"

She put her hand on my arm like a school nurse breaking the news that you're well enough to go back to class. "I can't. I've got a summer gig playing in the Hamptons. I leave this weekend."

"Oh," I said. I wasn't great at recovering from rejection.

"But maybe you could come catch my gig sometime, and we could go to the beach. I'm playing a little club called The Dock. It's in East Hampton."

Yeah, if I had a car or any way to get there. "You can

16

count on it," I said, my brain working furiously. Suki left, and as I trudged back to join Hakeem at our table, I could feel a boring summer weighing down on me. I was stuck interning at a girls' magazine. I had to spend time with my complete opposite, Lindsay DeWitt. And now I'd met a total babe who might as well be moving to Timbuktu.

"What's the word?" asked Hakeem.

"Know anybody who could give me a ride to the Hamptons this summer?" I asked without hope as we headed for the door.

"The only people I can think of with a summer place in the Hamptons would be rich people like Lindsay DeWitt and Alison Forrester," Hakeem said as the muggy night greeted us. "Guess you'll have to ask Lindsay."

I grimaced. "The day I drive to the Hamptons with Lindsay DeWitt is the day you can be sure I've been tortured and brainwashed."

TWO

Lindsay

I WAS ABOUT to hit the sack when my mom swooped through my bedroom door and gave me a big, smoochy kiss on the top of my head like she's done ever since I can remember. Her perfume hung on me for a minute, sweet, expensive, and fleeting.

"Hi, sweetie pea," she said in her throaty voice. "How was your day? Did you help out the lovelorn of America?"

For a minute I almost forgot to be mad at her. My mom had this way of waltzing in and making you feel so good, you just couldn't hold on to feeling angry. "It was fine," I said, trying to sound cold. "Up until the part where a certain blond lady I often share a house with decided to get engaged and announce it on TV before sharing the news with her only daughter."

"Oh, honey," my mom said, pulling me into her arms. I didn't hug back. "I kept trying to call you all day. Didn't you get my messages at the magazine?"

Oh yeah. The stack of messages that Lurlene, the *Blink* receptionist, had decided to let sit forever. Still, Mom should have waited to talk to me first. It made me feel like I was an afterthought. "You should have waited," I said, breaking away and crawling under my down comforter.

Mom sat down next to me and put both hands on either side of my cheeks. "Lindsay, baby," she started. "I am so sorry, but you weren't calling me back, and the station was pressuring me to make an announcement. We really wanted to scoop the *Post*. You're a writer. You understand that." The weird thing is, I did. And trying to stay mad at my mom was too much for me.

"I still wish you'd told me first. Everybody was totally grilling me about Jeffrey." I made a face. "And Alison."

"I'm so excited that you and Alison will get to know each other," Mom chirped. "She's really a sweetie. And it'll be like having the sister you always wanted."

"I wouldn't get your hopes up about Alison and me becoming the new Brady Bunch girls. She's got, like, this fierce clique she hangs out with. They're even cliquier than the other rich-kid cliques."

"She's been an absolute angel to me."

I so did not want to hear about my mom chumming it up with a girl whose face and habits sold magazines and gossip columns. Then again, my mom was a gossip-column item too, so it kind of made sense. I was the odd one out. "She doesn't even live here. Doesn't she go to some ultra-ultra school in Connecticut?"

"You sure do know a lot about her, for not caring."

"Whatever." I sniffed. I hate being busted by my mom.

"Well, the good news is that she's living with her father for the summer. Isn't that wonderful? We'll all have a chance to be a family together."

Yeah, great.

Then she dropped the real bomb. "Come on, Lindsay, outta that bed—it's only eight! And we're leaving in twenty minutes for a celebration dinner with Jeffrey and Alison!"

A door-size oil portrait of Alison hung over the monstrous stone fireplace in the Forresters' living room, which was in an even more ostentatious apartment building than my own. Portrait Alison, looking bored, wore Prada from head to toe and held a Chihuahua in her lap. Leave it to Alison Forrester to be immortalized on canvas with her cell phone at the ready. Ick.

"What do you think?" asked Jeffrey, blindsiding me. He handed me an expensive crystal wineglass filled with ginger ale. A little straw stuck out of the top of the glass.

"Oh," I said, trying to think fast. "The artist really captured Alison."

"You think so?" he said. "Well, she's my baby." He said it with such fatherly pride and love that I immediately felt bad about making fun of her. I tried to picture my dad on some yacht in the South of France, calling me his "baby." It would never happen, but I wished it would. Jeffrey put his arm around my shoulders. It was a surprisingly strong arm. "Lindsay, I know this is all kind of sudden, but I just want you to know that I love your mom and I plan to make her very happy. I hope you'll give us your blessing."

"Sure," I said, as if I could say anything else without starting a riot. I took a sip of my soda.

"Terrific."

A maid in uniform announced it was time for dinner.

Alison, on her ubiquitous cell phone, and her boyfriend, Marlon, appeared in the dining room as the first course was served. It was so strange to see Alison in person and not all glossy like in a magazine spread. "No," she said with drama. "No! No way . . . that is so contrabelievable . . . no. . . ." Marlon, the famous model, was trying to listen in. He'd get close, and she'd bat him away and turn her back.

"Ally, baby," Jeffrey said. "Tell Tiffany you'll call her back. We're having dinner. And we have *guests*."

Alison pursed her pretty pink lips and sighed. "Tiff? Gotta call you back late-ish. Yeah, we're having a family dinner," she said, emphasizing *family*. She looked over at me, then lowered her voice. "Yeah, I'll tell you more later."

Great. I was going to be topic number one on Alison's cell-phone agenda later. The evening was already shaping up to be a joy.

"So, Lindsay," Jeffrey said once we'd been served our soup. "Your mother says you're working at a magazine this summer?"

"Which magazine?" Marlon asked in his thick, northern British accent. *"Vogue? W? Vanity Fair?"*

"It's an online magazine called *Blink,*" I answered.

"Blink? Is it a magazine for eye doctors?" Marlon asked in all seriousness.

I shook my head. "It's a magazine for girls. You know, stuff about fashion. Boys. School. Music."

"Nerds," Alison said under her breath.

"Lindsay writes an advice column," my mom trilled. I knew she meant to break the ice, but I wished she'd just let it go so we could talk about something else, like mold spores. Any topic but my life would be fine.

"I think that's great," Jeffrey said, tearing off a hunk of bread. "It's good that teenagers have someone like you to help them out with their problems." It made me feel good to hear him say it. Truth was, I loved helping other people out with their boy troubles or school hang-ups. It was my own problems I couldn't face.

"That's so sweet," Alison said. She made it sound like a dirty habit. "And if you get good at it, you could probably write for one of the real magazines someday."

It's a good thing my butter knife was out of

23

reach. "It *is* a real magazine," I said, trying not to sound too defensive.

"I'm sure it's really cute. But it's not exactly *Vogue*. I'm in this month's issue."

"Isn't that great?" Jeffrey said. "Pretty terrific that both our girls are in the magazine business, right? I bet you two will be thick as thieves by the end of the summer."

Alison gave me a frosty smile. I glared back. Marlon was oblivious. "And don't forget my Fuel jeans ads. They'll be in lots of magazines this fall. Hey, do you think my bum looks too skinny in those pictures?"

The night dragged on like that. Mom and Jeffrey trying their best to make us into insta-family, just add water. Alison answering her phone a million times and giving people two-minute lowdowns about her whereabouts for the evening. Me trying to say as little as possible, and Marlon. Marlon might have been blessed with the beautiful strand of DNA, but when it came to smarts, he was hurting. By the time Jeffrey's housekeeper got around to serving us our main course, I was afraid I might be trapped there forever.

"I was thinking of making you girls my attendants," Mom gushed, tears springing to her eyes. She'd had a little too much wine. It made her happy and weepy at the same time. "But you could wear whatever you like."

"I know exactly what I'll wear," Alison said, resting her hand on her cell phone like she couldn't

24

bear to be away from it for too long. "I'm going straight to Calvin Klein and having them fit me for a pink, dupioni-silk strapless shift." Pink. The new black. Right.

"That sounds so beautiful," Mom said, edging more into tears category. "I love pink."

Marlon looked confused. "Riiight, the wedding. Oh, hey, I know some blokes got a great band back in Manchester. Sort of techno, but they mix in shop sounds, y'know, like saws and jackhammers and the like. Bleeding brilliant."

Jeffrey managed a smile. "We're planning quite a day-to-night extravaganza at Belle Reve, my Hamptons place. We'll start around 3 P.M. with a beach party—luau. Then we'll change for dinner and have the wedding and dancing till midnight."

Not only was my mom planning to go through with this ordeal, but now I was going to have to spend nine hours smiling and making nice to people I'd usually cross the street to avoid. Nine whole agonizing hours. Could it get any worse?

"So Lindsay," Alison said while the horror was still sinking in. "Who are you taking to the wedding?"

"Excuse me?" I said.

"Do you have a boyfriend?" she asked, like I was mentally retarded. "Or do you need us to hook you up with somebody appropriate?"

"No," I said defiantly. "I have a date."

"Really? Do we know him? Does he go to Choate? Poly Prep? It's not Piggy Binghamton, is it? We used to vacation with his family in Lucerne every year. He is so funny!"

"No," I said, starting to sweat a little bit. Where was I going to find a date? Someone to help me get through this thing? Did I even know any unattached guys?

"So," Alison said, leaning forward. "What's his name?"

"His name?" I repeated dumbly.

I don't know what came over me—call it temporary insanity of the nine-hour-wedding-date variety. Momentary desperation. A need to sock it right back to that snotty Alison. At any rate, I lost my marbles and said the only name that popped into my head.

"Daniel Newman."

Three

Daniel

"**H**AVE YOU BEEN sniffing the paste stick again?" I could not believe that Lindsay DeWitt was sitting in my cubicle, asking me to be her date to her mother's wedding. There had to be a punch line—probably with an actual punch.

She looked totally serious, a little miserable, and sort of cute as she put her finger to her lips in a "quiet" gesture. "Why don't you ask Biff or Skip or Chipwich or any of those other blue bloods who have pictures of the *Mayflower* in their living rooms? I don't get it."

Lindsay stared at her shoes like they might talk for her. "I sort of told my family you were already my date."

She leveled those deep brown eyes at me. Something inside me felt a little electric jolt, and I had this urge to make everything better for her. I don't know why.

"I couldn't help it," she said. "Everyone was going on about the wedding and dates, and they all looked at me like I was a dateless dork and . . . and besides, it'll just be the same dumb guys from the same families there, and I don't even want my mom to get married again, and . . . and I don't know what I'm saying. Just forget I asked, okay?"

I couldn't believe I was actually starting to feel sorry for the Debonator. Looking at her sitting on a step stool in my office, constantly pushing her hair behind her ears and having it fall forward again, I had a hard time seeing her with some big-trust-fund lug. At the same time I knew my dad would freak if I went to a society wedding as anything other than a gate-crasher for the revolution. "So, you're asking me to be your date to a nine-hour wedding that's only gonna be the most covered wedding of the year. What's my other choice—being forced to attend an 'N Sync concert with a group of screaming eight-year-old girls?"

"It's not going to be such a big deal," she said unconvincingly.

I picked up the morning's editions of the *Daily News* and the *New York Post*. "Let's see, this one says, 'The Wedding Belle Strikes Again.' And how about, 'Aisle Be Seeing You Again' in the *News*? Man, that is one bad headline."

"Look at it this way," she said. It's what she always said when we were arguing about a piece of advice in our column. I knew I was in for a tough fight. "You'll be front and center at one of the year's big news stories."

"No, a news story is something like war breaks out in East Slobovia or terrorists take over Disneyland."

"Terrorists take over Disneyland every year. They're called tourists with small children."

Man, she was quick. For a rich girl she had a pretty sharp sense of humor. But I wasn't giving in. "The point is," I said, "it would cause a certain amount of notoriety in my life. You know, pictures in the paper, people talking, wondering who I am—"

"Wondering if they should care . . ."

There are few things in life that smack your karma like getting dissed by a deb. Like who was she to dish out the 'tude when she was the one asking me to work a nine-hour date into my busy social schedule? Okay, so I wasn't *that* busy. "Sorry, DeWitt. No can do. Better luck elsewhere."

"Fine. Whatever." She sighed. "Where am I gonna find somebody for a nine-hour wedding in the Hamptons?"

Did she say *the Hamptons?* An idea started forming in my evil genius brain. A little tit for tat. Eye for an eye. Favor for a favor. A date for a ride. "Your mom's getting hitched in the Hamptons? Where, exactly?"

"Jeffrey has a place in East Hampton right on the beach. It's supposed to be nice, if you're into ten-thousand-square-feet mansions with fifteen-million-dollar views. Why?"

"Nothing," I lied. "Look, maybe I'm being too hard core about all this. I'm prepared to help you out on three conditions."

Lindsay narrowed her eyes at me.

I held up a finger. "One, you have to give me total access to you and Alison for the stupid *Blink* profile I have to do on you guys. Two, you help *me* this weekend with handing out flyers at a rally for the homeless that my dad's sponsoring. And three, when the wedding's over, I need a ride to a night-club in East Hampton."

Lindsay gave me her best I-smell-a-rat look. "What for?"

I shrugged, but my heart was beating like a high hat in a jazz band. "Just to listen to some cool music. No biggie. So do we have a deal?" I asked.

Lindsay flashed me a huge grin, which kind of knocked me off my feet at first. Like when you see somebody without glasses for the first time. She looked light and sparkly, the way my mom used to look when I brought home my art projects and she'd paste them on the fridge. I guess I'd just never noticed how pretty Lindsay was. She stopped smiling and started looking worried again. "Um, I think it would be a good idea if we didn't mention this to anyone here."

"Oh, right," I said sarcastically. "Wouldn't want anyone to think you were slumming. Consider it our secret."

"That's not what I meant," she snapped. "I just don't want to seem unprofessional here. Like if

30

people think we're dating, they'll start acting all weird around us and not taking us seriously."

I had to admit she had a point.

"Agreed," I said. "Now, how about Friday morning for our interview? Can you and Alison meet me in the lobby of her building at eleven o'clock?"

Lindsay got this funny look on her face, like she was smelling old gym socks. "Sure. I think so. I'll just ask my mom to call her dad."

"Why not just call her yourself? Correct me if I'm wrong, but you guys are about to be sisters, right?"

Lindsay gnawed her lower lip. "Eleven o'clock. We'll be there." It seemed like she was holding something back, like maybe she wasn't so hot on the ever-popular Miss Forrester. But who knows why girls do what they do? For all I knew, she could have been deciding whether to have caviar or lobster for lunch. Then the old DeWitt resurfaced. "By the way, your advice about Desperate in Des Moines? So off, it's not even funny."

"Excuse me," I said. "I think they *should* get back together. So the dude hates Valentine's Day. Big deal. Girls make too much out of it anyway."

"I knew you'd say that." She looked really pleased with herself. "So you think it's fine for a guy to just dump a girl, then try to get her back, all because he was too cheap to spring for a box of chocolates?"

This was more than an argument with my coauthor.

This was shaping up to be a fight to defend the honor of my fellow men. "Well, what did she get him for Valentine's Day, huh? You know, it goes both ways. Maybe he dumped her because she always made him foot the bill and he got tired of it."

"Forget it. I'm not having this argument with you. You clearly do not understand one thing about women." The Debonator turned around and stormed down the hall toward her cubicle.

"Oh yeah?" I called after her. "I do so know about women!" I stood there, pointing my finger at her disappearing back.

I did know a few things about women. I knew that Lindsay DeWitt was the most infuriating, impossible girl I'd ever met. I knew that Suki was the kind of girl who'd really understand me. And I knew that if you really loved someone, they could get sick and leave you forever one April morning while the sun was shining through a crystal prism in your hand, spreading small rainbows of color across your bedroom floor, and that was the last time you'd ever open your heart that wide again. I knew a few things about women. But I wished I didn't.

Lindsay

Daniel was due any minute to start his profile of Alison and me. I could see it all unfolding: Alison, the glamorous, carefree rich girl who was on the A-list for every hip party, and me, the girl who wore crew-neck, loose sweaters and liked to read a lot.

I'd chickened out on calling Alison myself. I asked Mom to ask Jeffrey, who, I was pretty sure, had blackmailed Alison into doing it by threatening to take away her manicure privileges. I just wanted the whole thing to be over. I tried to distract myself from the drama of it all by pulling out my laptop and focusing on somebody else's problems for a while. Jillian G. from Austin had sent *Blink* the following question:

> Dear Girl/Guy:
>
> Help! I've fallen for my worst enemy. T. and I have been total opposites forever. But now he's crushing on another girl, and I suddenly realize I'm in love with him. What should I do? Get him or forget him?
>
> Sincerely,
>
> Jillian G., Austin, Texas

I started tapping out an answer:

> Dear Jillian,
>
> Do you like him just 'cause he's got the hots for another girl? Or did it take another girl to make you realize you were in love all along?

Daniel's arrival in the lobby of the Forresters' building cut short my reply. As he dropped into a leather armchair next to me, I felt a teeny bit crushy

33

about Daniel. Huh? I was attracted to the Anti–Prince Charming? He was rude. He could barely find matching socks. He was totally impressed with himself.

He was also funny and smart and original—the only person I'd met in a long time who was just himself and wasn't putting on the big phony act. All the society kids I'd met tried to act like each other and dress alike. It was boring. With Daniel you never knew what you'd get, but you knew it would be one hundred percent him.

"So," he said, looking around the nearly empty lobby. "Where's Princess?"

"On her way down," I said. "I hear through the grapevine that she had a fight with her boyfriend, so maybe you should go kind of easy on her, okay?" I couldn't believe I was looking out for Alison. I was surprising myself all over the place today. But broken hearts had a way of getting to me.

Maybe Alison had something to do with my strange reaction to the sight of Daniel. There was *no* way he *wouldn't* be attracted to Alison, so maybe I was just attracted to him because I was jealous in advance?

Did that even make any sense?

Daniel flipped open a small notebook and jotted down a few notes. I was dying to see what he'd written. I was hoping it was something along the lines of: *11:00 A.M. Balmoral lobby. I am in the company of the devastatingly attractive and witty Miss Lindsay DeWitt. . . .* The flush started up again. I tried to make myself think about something unappealing like tuna-noodle casserole served by women in hair nets.

At eleven-thirty Alison finally put in her appearance. My heart sank immediately when I saw her glide from the elevator across the lobby in a formfitting blue dress and snappy high-heeled shoes that I would have broken my neck trying to walk in. Daniel stood up. The creep actually stood up when she reached the lobby. I'd never seen him stand up for anybody before—not even Ann. I wanted him to die.

"Sorry, I couldn't find my sunglasses," she said, pushing a pair of Gucci cat's-eye frames up onto her pert nose.

Alison and Daniel nodded at each other, then we piled into a taxi, Daniel up front with the driver, Alison and me in the back. Alison had made reservations at a fancy Japanese restaurant.

"So what do you think about your dad marrying Lindsay's mom?" Daniel asked, turning around to face us as the taxi sped downtown.

"I think it's great," Alison said. "My mom's remarried, and he's been single for a long time. And Caroline is really nice and very stylish."

"So," Daniel said. "You and Lindsay will be sisters. What's that gonna be like?"

"I'm just starving!" I cut in, hoping it wasn't too obvious that I didn't want her to answer that question.

"Great, because we're here," Alison said in a bored tone.

Sashimi was the trendiest sushi place in Manhattan. Autographed pictures of Leo DiCaprio and Winona Ryder smiled down at us from walls painted a minimalist gray. We took off our shoes and sat cross-legged on floor pillows around a low table. Alison ordered about a dozen different kinds of raw fish for the table. Not being wild about slimy food, I ordered some vegetable tempura so I wouldn't starve. Plus I'm not good with chopsticks, and having fish-rice product dangling from your mouth definitely makes the unattractive list.

Daniel took a big bite of hamachi and launched into his questions. "So, Alison, who are your best buds? I mean, who do you hang with?"

"Tiffany Ledbetter, Cornelia Higgins, Sarah Jane Wynne, Kim Yamaguchi, Astrid Grubener . . . and those are just the girls."

"Whoa. No wonder you need such a big apartment. What about you, DeWitt? Who are your nearest and dearest?"

Our waiter filled our water glasses, saving me from admitting that I had only one friend (Maggie Irving), who was a counselor-in-training at a sleepaway camp for the summer. "Most of my friends are pretty publicity shy," I said. "I don't want to embarrass them or anything. Hey, does anyone want any of this veggie tempura? It's pretty good," I added, hoping to change the subject.

Alison wrinkled her nose. "It's fried. You cannot even imagine the fat content on that plate." Alison's cell phone went off in her purse. She grabbed it. "Hello? Yes, Astrid, Marlon and I are sooo over. Yeah, I know I said that last week, but this time I mean it. So, what's our MO for tonight . . . uh–huh . . ."

"I'll try your tempura." Daniel grabbed a fork and speared a big piece of crispy eggplant. "Hey, DeWitt, what about your dad?"

"What about him?" The question caught me off guard.

"What's his deal? I mean, do you ever see him?"

I stared at my greasy plate and thought about the last time I'd seen my dad. He'd flown in at Christmastime with his new wife and their baby, Miles. We went to FAO Schwarz to see the rows and rows of beautiful stuffed bears, looking for just the right one for Miles, who was all smiles. Dad picked up an alligator puppet and pretended to grab Miles's nose again and again, sending him into squeals of delight. It made me feel so incredibly sad, wishing my dad would do something stupid like tweak *my* nose or tickle *my* sides. I just wanted to see that look of joy on his face when he looked at me. We bought Miles a huge panda with a pink tongue, and Dad gave me a collection of e. e. cummings poems. It was the same book he'd gotten me two years before, but I didn't say anything except thanks.

"Earth to Lindsay," Daniel said through a mouthful of eggplant.

I shoved the plate toward the middle of the table. "Yeah, I see him. He lives in England, but we see each other on holidays."

"What does he think about your mom getting hitched for the fifth time?"

"I wouldn't know," I said testily. I could tell Daniel was enjoying his status as interrogator. "You make it sound like it's a disease or something."

"Well, you've gotta admit, five times is more than the average, right?"

"What about your parents? Are they still together? Divorced? Remarried?" I crossed my arms and stared at him. He got this look on his face. It wasn't the usual smart-alecky Daniel smirk. He looked more like a lost puppy, and I wished I hadn't sounded so harsh.

"I'm asking the questions here," he said in a hard tone. It seemed like the only time I opened my mouth was to put my feet inside it.

"Okay, sweetie. Love you too," Alison said, air kissing into her phone and hanging up. "What did I miss?"

"Apparently Lindsay doesn't want to talk about her friends, her parents, or any other aspect of her life. Guess we'll have to make up the answers," Daniel said with a satisfied smile. I could have kicked him.

Alison giggled. "So are you guys dating or what?" she asked, forking a single piece of rice into her mouth. "I mean, you're going to the wedding together, right?"

I felt my tempura doing flip-flops in my stomach. Was Alison hitting on Daniel? He couldn't possibly be her type!

"We're going as friends," I said quickly before he could.

Alison eyed me, then turned her attention to Daniel. "So, Daniel," she said, handing her platinum Visa card to a waiter. "Daddy suggested I invite you and Lindsay to the pool party we're having this weekend. You'll get insight into the life of Alison Forrester for your little article, and we'll all have a chance to get to know Daniel before the wedding. It's this Sunday, starting around two. Bring a towel."

I could think of nothing more loathsome than spending the day with Daniel and Alison at a pool party. Root canal. Upper-lip wax.

The credit-card slip signed, Alison excused herself to get her hair highlighted. I figured Daniel would want to annoy me with more questions, but he bagged too.

"Well, guess I'll get in some b-ball while the sun's still shining," Daniel said. "See you Sunday by the pool."

I didn't want to spend time with him either. Well, not really. But couldn't he have at least pretended to be interested in hanging out for another hour to discuss his slant for the article or something?

Four

Daniel

ON SATURDAY MORNING my dad caught me staring at my bare chest in the full-length mirror attached to the bathroom door. He raised an eyebrow.

"A girl invited me to a pool party tomorrow," I explained. "I'm doing a profile on her for *Blink*. It's Alison Forrester."

Dad jolted like he'd been shot out of a cannon. "Jeffrey Forrester's daughter?"

I nodded and prepared for the lecture.

"The Forresters live in a whole different world from you and me, Daniel. Sure, go and have a good time. Just don't think *that's* what real life is. Real life is about good grades. Internships. Getting into a good college. Making something of yourself. Real life doesn't happen on Fifth Avenue."

Why couldn't he just once say, *Gee, that's great,*

son. Have fun. Here's twenty bucks while you're at it.

"Anyway, son, don't forget about the homeless rally today. Three o'clock. Tompkins Square Park. I believe you said you had a friend to help out."

"I'll be there," I assured him, disappearing into my bedroom to call the Debonator and call in my marker for the rally. I punched in her digits. She answered on the second ring.

"Hey, DeWitt," I said. "It's your conscience calling. My dad's rally is today."

"I'll be there," she said. There was no recognizable attitude or anything. It was so weird. "What time?"

"The rally's at three." Suddenly I didn't feel like being alone in my apartment. Hakeem was away for the weekend, and I wasn't in the mood to hang out at The Coffeehouse by myself. "So, I think we should meet at two, just in case my dad needs us for prep."

"Sure," she said in a perky voice. It was what my mom used to call my guilty voice. Like after I'd used her lipstick to paint my model airplane red and she asked if I knew where it was, I'd get that happy tone to my voice to ward off suspicion. I didn't know what made me think of that.

We'd arranged to meet in front of the park, and we both showed up five minutes early. I'd never met a girl who was not only on time but early. It kind of threw me. She was wearing her usual uniform of J. Crew khakis and some kind of tasteful white shirt. Her ponytail bounced when she

42

walked. With her sunglasses and the peppy pony-tail, she could've posed for one of those I'd-rather-be-sailing posters. She looked really cute, in that classy, Jackie-O.-in-training sort of way. Usually seeing DeWitt set my teeth on edge, but after the stuff with my dad that morning, it was sort of soothing to see her.

We walked over to the table my dad had set up, and I introduced Lindsay, avoiding her last name. Dad handed us a stack of flyers and told us to stake out the far corner.

"Mr. Newman?" Lindsay said. "Maybe Daniel and I should stand over by the playground, where a lot of parents are, since they're the heart of the community."

I wondered what Mr. Rigid would say to a good idea like that. "Smart thinking," he told Lindsay, nodding in the Dad-seal-of-approval motion. "Hit the playground, then."

Lindsay and I took our flyers and stood at the gated entrance to the playground, handing flyers to parents coming in with their strollers and kids in tow. Lindsay and I were so busy trying to convince people to take a flyer that we barely had time to talk to each other.

At five, the end of our shift, we handed our left-over flyers (not many) to my dad, who thanked us both for our help. When I mentioned that I was going to walk Lindsay to the subway station, my dad pointedly reminded me that he expected me home for dinner by six.

"So thanks for coming and all," I told Lindsay as we headed out of the park. "Guess you only owe me one last favor now."

"I know—a ride to that club in East Hampton," Lindsay said as we walked down the steps to the Astor Place subway station.

"So, is everything okay with your dad?" she asked, eyeing me. "Or is he just really into timely dinners?"

"He's just wound a little tight," I replied. The conversation was going in a direction I didn't want to travel. The afternoon with the Debonator had been surprisingly nice, and I wasn't ready to get into a big heavy mood.

A train came rumbling by. The wind-tunnel effect blew open my notebook, and out flew the flyer Suki had given me for her gig. Lindsay caught it. She pretended not to notice, but I knew she'd looked pretty hard at Suki's come-hither pose on the flyer. I was pretty sure she'd also seen the address for the gig in the Hamptons.

The doors on the six train binged open. "Gotta run," Lindsay said, shoving the flyer at me.

Busted.

Lindsay

Jeffrey had secured his building's rooftop pool for the afternoon. The pool was inside under a glass roof, and there was a big terrace with lots of tables and benches and planters just outside. I sat on a teak

44

bench and felt like an idiot in my dark green tank-ini. I'd thought I was so daring wearing a two-piece, even if it did cover my navel, until all of Alison's friends started showing up in these tiny bikinis with enough foam padding to fill a mattress. There was definitely no shortage of cleavage, except for me. I was there to fill the small-cup quota.

"Sugar, can you bring me my lemonade?" Alison called to Marlon from the diving board, where she was perched on the edge, kicking water at a couple of big, beefy guys. Alison had run into Marlon at a club the night before, and now they were all lovey-dovey again. The nausea factor was heavy. Marlon looked pretty perfect in his surf shorts. I guessed that was why he was a model.

I slathered on some sunblock, hoping it would help block out my mopey feelings about Daniel and the singer. Suki. Her name was Suki. And she was stone-cold gorgeous.

Wait a minute. What was wrong with me? This was Daniel Newman we were talking about, not Prince William. We were totally wrong for each other, all the way. To prove it to myself, I took a small scrap of paper from my tote bag and started listing reasons we were not meant to be.

He has a huge ego.

He likes girls with names like Suki who sing in bands.

My heart stopped as Daniel stepped out of the elevator doors in loud, striped swim shorts down to his knees and a T-shirt that read Mean People Taste

Just Like Chicken. He had a beach towel slung over his shoulder and an old pair of Ray-Ban sunglasses on his Roman nose. I had never been so happy to see somebody. Finally, someone at this stupid party I could relate to.

Wait a minute. Huh? What was going on here?

Daniel was looking around—for me, I figured. I shoved the paper I'd been scribbling on into my tote bag as his gaze landed on me. He waved and headed over. I leaned back on the bench a bit, trying to adopt a cool pose.

"Hey," he said, plopping down next to me but not seeming to notice my near-naked splendor at all. "Come on, DeWitt. Let's take a dip."

He grabbed my hand, and I had a hard time catching my breath. I let him drag me into the pool area. "Should I go in first? Or should *you!*" With a quick push he jettisoned me into the pool. The cool water felt great. I got Daniel back by pushing his shoulders underwater. He surfaced and grinned, chasing after me in shark mode.

Then we sank to the bottom and sat, Buddha style, waiting to see who could hold their breath the longest. After the longest minute of my life Daniel broke for the surface, and I followed in his bubbly wake. When we resurfaced, everyone had moved out to the terrace, where food was being served.

Daniel looked around. "Gee, were we having too much fun for everyone?"

Yes. We were. "Come on," I said, swimming for

the side. "We don't want to miss the food."

As we surfaced by the ladder out of the pool, we bumped bodies. Daniel smelled like fresh sheets and chlorine and something totally musky and him. I wanted to bury my nose in his chest. For a split second I glanced up into Daniel's endless, blue-horizon eyes and got lost. Then he was kissing me under the hot sun. His lips were soft and warm against mine. I could hear my blood throbbing in my temples. And then he moved back from me.

"Whoa. Sorry. I didn't mean to do that."

Of course not. Kissing me would have to be a mistake. Tears pricked at my eyes, but I refused to cry. "It's okay. No biggie."

"Gee, thanks for the ringing endorsement," he said. "You really know how to make a guy feel great."

Well, he hadn't exactly been Romeo himself. What did he expect? "Look, it was just the moment, okay?" I lied. "You didn't mean to do it, and neither did I."

"Fine, whatever," he said, climbing out of the pool. He walked off toward the buffet, grabbing a towel and slinging it around his neck.

Now I was really angry. "You know, you are so rude," I hissed, walking after him. We were standing at the end of the food line.

He whipped around to face me. "I'm rude? You just totally dissed me in the pool. Excuse me, Your Highness. Maybe we should forget about this whole date-for-a-ride arrangement."

"Fine with me," I snapped.

"Fine!"

With that he stalked off into the elevator.

My lips were still tingly from his kiss, and already I had lost him.

Five

Lindsay

I'D SPENT SUNDAY night crying into my favorite stuffed animal. On Monday at *Blink,* I'd avoided Daniel for fear of bursting into tears at the sight of him, and he avoided me too. I couldn't stop thinking of our fight or his expression as he'd stalked off yesterday afternoon. And as if I wasn't torturing myself enough, I kept remembering his kiss. I'd never experienced anything so intense and totally sweet at the same time. Like at that moment I stopped worrying about my stupid tankini, my thighs, my mom marrying Jeffrey Forrester, my life and just surrendered to being happy. And then I had to go and screw it up. Maybe I just wasn't cut out for being a normal girl doing normal girl things. But I wanted that more than anything.

I'd stopped home after work to cry in private

and freshen up so that my mom wouldn't know anything was wrong. I was supposed to meet Mom at the TV station, where she was doing her piece at five-thirty, and then we were going to have dinner. I grabbed the day's mail and jumped into a cab on Fifth Avenue. Most of the mail was for Mom, but there was a postcard for me from the South of France. It was a small, glossy picture of boats against an orangy sunset. I flipped it over and read the familiar handwriting.

> *Dearest Lindsay,*
>
> *I hope you are well and having a good summer vacation. We are enjoying our holiday here in Monte Carlo. Miles loves the beaches. Veronique and I are getting great tans. Perhaps we'll come here together over Christmas? We're on to Italy next. I'll ring you when we return to England.*
>
> *Lovingly,*
> *Your father*

There was a hard patch forming at the back of my throat, and then the front seat of the taxi went all blurry, and I realized I was crying again. I looked out the window at the tourists bustling along the busy streets with their families and wished I could be part of a family like that: mothers telling daughters not to brush their hair in public, fathers putting arms around kids' shoulders and pointing out the Empire State Building on a cheesy map, brothers and sisters getting underfoot and in your hair. It seemed like I was the one telling my parents to grow up. Just once I wanted to be bad. I wanted to know they were huddled in the living room together, wringing their hands over what to do with their precious problem child.

Mom was getting her makeup done when I arrived at the television station. Carly, the makeup artist, flitted around my mom, dusting her with powder. Mom looked up from her notes and saw me in the big, lighted mirror.

"Hi, sweetie, come on in. How was your day?"

"Okay." I sighed.

"Hmmm, that doesn't sound okay."

I just didn't want to go into it and have Mom get all upset and start in on her there-must-be-something-wrong-with-him-if-he-doesn't-realize-what-a-wonderful-prize-you-are speech. I think they learn that in mom training school as the stock answer to all teen-girl misery. Fortunately fate intervened in the form of the assistant producer, who stuck his head in the door.

"We need you, Caroline."

Mom jumped up from her chair, gave me a kiss, and pulled me out on the set to watch her tape the night's consumer-reports piece on the best local florists. Afterward she taped one more segment on the best pedicures in town, then headed back to her dressing room to wash her face. I liked smelling all her face soaps and watching her get all lathery. "So, Lindsay Loo," she said from behind a soapy face. "Are you going to tell me what's bothering you? Or do I have to torture you for the information?"

I rolled my eyes. "Mom, I'm not five anymore. I think the statute of limitations on the tickling torture ends at ten."

Mom splashed water on her face and toweled off. "Ve haf vays of making you talk."

"It's no big deal," I said. "Really." She gave me a skeptical gaze and slathered some cream on her cheeks. I picked up a small, handprint paperweight on Mom's desk. I'd made it for her in camp when I was five. "Mom, do I have to bring a date to the wedding?"

She sat next to me on the small brown love seat. She put her arm around my shoulders and hugged me. "I thought you were taking that boy from the magazine. David."

"Daniel," I said, feeling slightly annoyed that she couldn't remember his name.

"Right, Daniel. What happened?"

"We sort of had a fight."

Mom walked over to her dressing table and began dabbing cream under her eyes. "Well, if he's not smart enough to realize what a prize you are, then I say good riddance." She'd gone right for the stock answer. Zero to sixty in nothing flat.

I lay back on the love seat and stared at the track lighting in the ceiling. "It's not that. The fight was my fault. Anyway, the point is, he's totally out of the picture, and there's nobody I want to go with. Besides, it's not like it matters if I go alone. Everybody's there to see you and Jeffrey." And

Alison and Marlon. And Lindsay, the dateless freakish wonder. Of course it mattered. It mattered a lot. But I felt like wallowing in my aloneness.

Mom picked up her phone and punched a number on her speed dial. I couldn't figure out who she could be calling in the middle of my teen crisis. As far as I knew, there was no such service as rent-a-boy. And even if there were, I'd die before I'd call them. Mom brushed pinky brown blush over the apples of her cheeks, changing the phone from ear to ear to accommodate the makeup routine. "Hi, honey. It's me." Honey. It had to be Jeffrey. "Listen, I know a certain wonderful young lady who could use a date to a wedding." I couldn't believe what I was hearing. It was like watching the heroine walk up the dark stairs in a horror movie when you want to scream, "Stop," but you can't.

"Mom!" I hissed in a loud whisper, and shook my head no ferociously. Mom turned her back and walked over to the minifridge to get some water.

"Uh-huh . . . uh-huh . . . oh, he sounds terrific!" She turned and winked at me. I wondered if I had time to join the Peace Corps and ship out before the wedding. Mom went on in a flirty voice. "I miss you too. Yes. Okay, honey. See you then. And thanks for the Prince Charming bit." She made a kissing noise into the phone. There are few things more mortifying than having to listen to your mom get all sugary sweet with her boyfriend. Except for having to listen to your mom beg her boyfriend to find you a suitable date. I could just imagine what Alison would say when she found out I needed a setup. Great.

Daniel

"Don't get attached," my buddy Jack said as he, Hakeem, and I found seats at The Coffeehouse on Monday night. "Do the leaving, not the grieving."

"Correct me if I'm wrong, Jack," I said, "but when Dana Rosenman broke up with you after three weeks, didn't you stand outside her homeroom class every day till she asked you never to talk to her again?" I grinned at Hakeem, who put his hand up to his mouth to keep from laughing.

Jack got on his I-refuse-to-let-you-know-I'm-ticked-off face. "Listen, the point is, you did the right thing, Newman. Dump her. Quick. Painless. Easy. Like pulling off a Band-Aid."

I stopped laughing and thought about Lindsay's face when I told her I thought we should forget the date-for-a-ride arrangement. It had been anything but painless. The fact was, part of me wanted to spend nine hours with her at her mother's wedding. Part of me did want to kiss her again. To feel her kiss me back. "We were never dating, so it wasn't really a dump."

"Whatever. Pass the sugar."

"Hi. It's Dabney, right?" I followed the sound of that soft, raspy voice up to the perfect, heart-shaped face of Suki. She was wearing a rose-print dress and an old buckskin jacket that was big enough to be her dad's. I couldn't speak. Couldn't even breathe. My belly was doing high-dive flops. My heart whispered, *I love you.* I hoped my mouth had been shut.

Jack smacked me back to reality with a jab on the arm. "How's it going, Dabney?"

"Daniel," I said, standing up quickly and knocking over my chair. *Someone please shoot me.* I pulled up the chair and offered it to her.

"No thanks. I can't hang."

"So, what are you doing back in the city?" I asked, seeing the two of us arm in arm at a movie tomorrow night.

"I just came by to drop off some more flyers." She showed me a stack of purple paper about half an inch thick.

"Oh, hey. I could take some of those for you. Drop 'em off at my office. It's an Internet magazine."

"Cool." Her eyes lit up. "Do they have a music-review section?"

"Yeah, they do."

She bit her bottom lip, a move I have never been able to resist. "Do you think you could pass on my CD to them? It would be really cosmic if I could get some coverage."

I would have done anything for her. Sleep in the desert. Wear an I'm with Stupid shirt. I didn't know yet how far I'd have to go to make good on that promise. "You bet," I said, taking the CD, instantly wishing I'd said something about being the music reviewer myself instead of "you bet" like a Boy Scout. "So are these the flyers for your gig in the Hamptons?"

"Yeah. I'm playing out there on July 29. I don't

come on till midnight, which is a pretty cruddy time. But it is a Saturday, so you could always sleep in the next morning." She gave me a sideways glance. "You will come, won't you?"

How could I say no? Saturday the twenty-ninth sounded really familiar, and I remembered just as Jack did.

"Hey, dude, isn't that the same night as DeWitt's mom's wedding? You have got it made."

Sure, if only I hadn't told Lindsay our deal was off. I was beyond stuck. I was buried. Suki's CD burned in my hand. There was only one thing to do. I had to get Lindsay to take me back as her date. Talk about your mission impossible. Then again, if she wanted a date as much as I wanted a ride to the gig, maybe the fact that Lindsay and I couldn't get along wouldn't matter.

"I'll be there," I said. She kissed me on the cheek and waved bye-bye using only her fingers.

"Ooh, Dabney! I'm in love!" Jack fell off his chair. I stepped over him and sat to ponder my wicked predicament.

Hakeem said it all. "Dan, my man, you are in some serious straits."

I watched Suki glide across the floor and hand her CD to the guy behind the counter. She was everything I'd ever claimed I wanted. And *she* wanted me to come to her gig. I'd be a fool not to go. I took a sip of Jack's leftover coffee and tried not to face the fact that being a fool was kind of my specialty these days.

I had to get to Suki's gig. Even if it meant making nice to the girl who'd just burned me.

56

Six

Lindsay

I BARELY PREPARED for my first date with Price Winston III and was barely ready when Mom called me down to meet my doom. He was standing at the bottom of the stairs. Tall. Black hair. Shoulders you could rest the world on. And a face right out of *GQ*. It was like he'd been ordered from a catalog. Go, Mom.

Jeffrey came out of the living room. "Price, I'd like you to meet Lindsay. Lindsay, this is Price. He's going to take really good care of you tonight. Aren't you, Price?"

The friendly threat was a little over the top, but Price didn't break a sweat. "Absolutely."

He wore a jacket and a button-down shirt. I doubted Daniel Newman even owned a jacket. But I wasn't going to think about Daniel tonight. That was over. A mistake. A crazy idea of mine that thankfully had not seen the light of day. My future lay with Price Winston III. We would be the talk of the wedding.

After some drawn-out good-byes (I'd managed to talk Mom out of one picture for the photo album . . . sooo embarrassing . . .) Price and I were standing on the front steps of my town house. I could feel Mom, Jeffrey, and Consuela peeking out at us from behind the living-room drapes.

We walked to a guarded parking lot where Price led me to his SUV. He did that beep-beep thing with his door-unlocking remote device and helped me pile into the passenger seat. "Boy, you are so lucky." He said it out loud, but it was almost like he was talking to himself.

"How do you figure that?" I asked.

"Getting Jeffrey Forrester for a father-in-law. You can have anything you want. I'd love to work for Mr. Forrester. Apprentice under him till I was about thirty, then call it a day." We pulled out onto Fifth Avenue and cruised toward the park.

A creepy feeling made its way up my spine. I shooed it away. "What would you do after that?"

He looked at me like I'd sprouted two heads. "Retire. What else?"

"At *thirty?* Isn't that kind of young? Wouldn't you get bored?"

"No way. I'd make use of my time."

"Doing what?" I thought of him volunteering with the Red Cross or starting an experimental school for kids, his strong hands leaning in to help rescue a cat stuck in a tree during a flash flood in Boise.

"Golf," he answered. "I would love to get my game under one hundred. Oh, hey, do you like the Dave Matthews Band?"

"Not really," I said, feeling suddenly edgy and uncomfortable.

Price popped a CD into the car stereo and adjusted the volume. "I think you'll like this. Just give it a listen. You gotta love Dave Matthews."

I didn't love Dave Matthews. And I didn't love guys who insisted I needed to love Dave Matthews. I wondered how we'd get through the evening, just the two of us, if it was starting out on such a sour note.

Price steered us into valet parking for his father's club and then up to a big room where a party was in full swing. "You don't mind stopping in to see a few of my friends, do you?" Before I could answer, two big guys rushed him. They all tackled each other and shouted mock insults in the testosterone equivalent of an epileptic fit.

"Mark. John. I want you to meet Lindsay DeWitt. Her mom's the one marrying Jeffrey Forrester."

I shook hands with the goon squad and mumbled nice-to-meet-yous. We mingled with the "in" crowd. Mostly Price mingled and I sat in a chair, watching my ginger-ale glass get all sweaty on the outside. Occasionally he'd wave or wink at me from another part of the room. I wished Daniel were there to help me laugh and feel more comfortable. Mark the Goon offered to refill my glass. "Do you go to St. Ann's?"

"No," I said, tucking my hair behind my ears. "The Magnet School."

"Oh," he said, shaking his head up and down. "That's that artsy school downtown, right?"

"I guess."

"How come you don't go to St. Ann's or Hockney Day School or Spence? It's not like you can't afford it."

"It isn't about money. Magnet has a great writing program, and there are a lot of international kids who go there. It's really cool. In one of my classes there's a girl from India, a guy from Botswana, another guy from Saudi Arabia—"

"Great. Bunch of foreigners using our schools. You should go to St. Ann's. The really fine girls go there." He looked me up and down like a three-course meal. So not attractive. Price walked up, and he and Mark mock wrestled again. What is it with guys and the physical contact disguised as sports?

"You're not moving in on my date, are you, buddy?"

"Hey, man. You were over there. Tough luck, Winst."

Price threw a soft punch, and Mark pretended to go limp. If I had to spend another hour here, I'd start looking for a hidden stash of cyanide somewhere. Mark backed off. "I heard Jeffrey's about to open some casinos. Should net him enough to send you to Spence or something. Hey, Price, did you know Lindsay's going to that weirdo Magnet School?"

"Really?"

You'd think I'd just said I sold stray cats to the local meat-pie shop. "My mom and I believe in the importance of meeting all kinds of people and getting a really great education." I was feeling pretty steamed.

"Your mom's a little . . . different, isn't she?" He'd said *different* like it was a dirty word.

"What do you mean?"

"Keep your shirt on. She's cool. But you know, married to Jeffrey Forrester, she'll kind of need to rein it in a bit. I doubt Forrester would let his stepkid go to The Magnet School."

Would my mother suddenly listen to everything Jeffrey said? Would she pull me out of my school? Make me become like Alison? Force me on dates with guys like Price? Suddenly I couldn't see my mom—me—us—happy in this kind of life. When my mom had gotten married before, she'd gotten into everything from wearing Navajo ponchos to riding motorcycles. What would happen when she fell in with Jeffrey and Alison Forrester and all these horrible people? It was totally beyond reality.

I had to stop it. I had to keep Mom from making a huge mistake.

But how?

I could help Mom see the truth about Jeffrey's world before it was too late.

But that was equal to derailing the wedding. *Could* I do that? *Should* I do that?

All I did know was that when you were even thinking about plotting a crime, you needed to find a criminal mind. And the most criminal mind I could think of belonged to Daniel Newman.

Daniel

So anyway, I forgive you, and all I'm asking in return is that you drop me off at The Dock at midnight in East Hampton to meet my true love. I stared at myself in the steamy bathroom mirror. "Yeah, Dan," I said to myself. "That's really gonna work. *Not.*"

I'd called the Debonator and asked her to meet me at Central Park for a sit-down. She seemed really surprised to hear from me, and she'd surprised me by saying she wanted to talk to me too. All morning long and on the subway ride up to the park I'd gone over what I'd say to her. We'd agreed to meet at the carousel in the park (her idea). So, the plan was: Meet DeWitt. Get back on the wedding trail. Ask for ride. Ba-da-bing. Ba-da-bang. Ba-da-boom. Over and out.

Lindsay was sitting on a bench near the carousel when I got there, and I felt my breath catch in my chest a little. She was the polar opposite of Suki, the girl of my dreams, and still . . . suddenly I was back to thinking about the kiss. I had to get over it.

"Hey," I said, bumping her with my elbow as I sat down next to her. "What's up?"

"I don't know. You're the one who called me, so you go first."

I went through the whole gee-I've-given-this-a-lot-of-thought spiel and told her I was over being mad. "So we're on for the wedding, right?"

She stared at me. "How do you know *I'm* not over being mad and don't already have another date lined up?"

I hadn't even thought about the new-date possibility. I scoffed as best I could even though my mouth was dry from fear. "With who?"

Lindsay stared at the horses going round and round. It seemed like an eternity passed before she said, "Okay, I don't have another date. But there's not going to be a wedding. Not if I can help it."

I rest my case about girls being eternal mysteries. "Wait a minute," I said. An uncomfortable feeling was inching up my spine. Panic. That was the word I was searching for. "Two days ago you were all over the idea. What's the deal?"

"The deal is that Jeffrey is all wrong for my mom. I don't know. I can't explain it. I just . . ." She trailed off, and for a minute I was afraid she was going to cry. The Debonator crying was not something I thought I could handle. She got very quiet. "I can't see us sitting in club rooms with those same empty people, talking about clothes and trips, who's in, who's out. He's bad for her. And I loathe Alison. There, I said it. Do you think I'm a bad person?"

"No," I said. I meant it. "I just don't understand how I can help you jinx your mom's wedding."

"By the time I'm done, that see-through billionaire and his fashion-slave daughter will think I'm so horrible that they won't want to be associated with us. I can't be truly horrible without your guidance."

"Gee, thanks, DeWitt. Remind me to boost your ego sometime."

"Believe it or not, it's actually a compliment. Why do you think I suggested meeting at my favorite place?"

"So this is your favorite place," I said, watching little kids going round and round and up and down on painted horses while calliope music blared out of the speakers. I'd lived in New York all my life and never once been on the thing.

Lindsay was practically throwing her quarters at the ticket lady. "Let's see if Moonbeam is open."

Moonbeam turned out to be a black stallion with bared teeth. I rode the gray mare next to him. The sucker went pretty fast. I could only imagine that disgruntled parents used it to scare their kids into submission. Lindsay leaned back, let go of the pole, and let the wind pull her hair behind her. I closed my eyes and did the same. It was amazing. When I opened my eyes; Lindsay was beaming at me. "Cool, huh?"

Very cool. The ride slowed down just as I was finally getting the hang of it. When it came to a stop, we exited through the big wooden gate and found an ices stand a few yards away. We sat on a big rock next to some afternoon sun worshipers and ate our ices.

"You know," I said, trying to keep my frozen lemon mound from melting over the side of the paper cup and down my arm. "You're not as spoiled as I thought you'd be."

Lindsay laughed. "The compliment god strikes again! I may swoon."

"You know what I mean."

"No, I don't. Do I have a big dollar sign on my forehead or something?"

"Okay, so I'm not smooth. It's just that all the rich girls I've ever met were like Alison—spoiled, superficial, snotty."

"My mom has a big heart. She wanted me to grow up to be part of the world, not to rule it. That's why she sent me to an arts school and introduced me to lots of different people and cultures and things. It's why I want to be a writer."

"Admit it, you'd rather date a rich guy than an average guy."

"That is so not true. You understand nothing about girls, Daniel. Seriously."

"Okay, great love goddess advice woman, what don't I understand?"

Lindsay licked a soupy glob of ice off her hand. "Look, a guy could give me a silly homemade card and totally win me over. It's about thought. It's about knowing what the girl wants—not what the guy wants to do and gee, guess the girl better just like it." She was working up to a pretty good indignant lather when a slow smile crept across her face. It made me nervous. "I challenge you."

"What?"

"I, Lindsay DeWitt, challenge you, Daniel Newman, to a contest of wits. A dating contest. I'll take you out on the perfect girl's date, and you show me a perfect guy's date. We'll see which one is more fun."

Once my best friend, Kenny, threw a curveball when I was up at bat. I knew it was a curveball. I heard it. Smelled it, even. Saw it coming. But I hit anyway and struck out. I knew what Lindsay had just hurled my way was a wicked curveball. I knew any girl who could ride Moonbeam with no hands was gonna be a tough competitor. But I was game. I stood at home plate and took aim.

"You're on, DeWitt."

Seven

Lindsay

MYSTERY DATE. THAT'S all I could think about.

My mom used to have this cheeseball board game from the sixties called Mystery Date. You'd take your turn, then open one of three doors to reveal either a hottie yachtsman or a total train wreck of a loser. As I slipped into my black dress and Mom's silver beaded sweater for my "perfect date" with the unpredictable Mr. Newman, I prayed I'd open the door to find a Daniel who'd at least changed out of his holey jeans and T-shirt.

I was standing on the sidewalk outside City Center, holding tickets for the American Ballet Theater's performance of *Swan Lake*. It was ten minutes till curtain time, and there was still no sign of him. All around me well-dressed old women in gobs of jewelry walked arm in arm with their tuxedoed husbands and inside the theater. The tickets were getting droopy from my sweaty palms.

"Hey, you're not scalping those, are you?" Daniel came running up from the other side of the street, nearly getting creamed by a cab. My Mystery Date door opened to a view of a major babe in a crisp shirt and tie, jacket, khakis, and . . . high-top sneakers. It was a start.

"Come on," I said, pulling him into the lobby and up the stairs before he could protest. "I hate being late."

We got our programs and settled into our box seats—courtesy of Mom, who gave lots of money to the arts. "So what's the plan about your mom's wedding?"

I took a quick look around to make sure there was no one I knew within earshot. "Here's the deal: Tomorrow we're getting together with the Forresters. I plan to be as scary as possible. That's where you come in."

Daniel arched an eyebrow. "That's where I come in and what? Ransack the place? Take a hostage?"

"No. Just show up wearing that Eat the Rich T-shirt you love so much. It couldn't hurt to mention your dad's name. We'll both be totally obnoxious. I know you can do that." I smiled and patted his hand.

Daniel zigzagged his hand away from my touch. "Seems like you don't need any pointers from me on that score."

"Look," I said, lowering my voice to a whisper. "If Jeffrey thinks we're wacky communist-terrorist types, maybe he'll get cold feet. Or try to send me to Switzerland to paramilitary ski camp or something just as dire, and Mom will be over him." The lights flickered, faded, and darkened to a shadow, and the ballet began. I glanced nervously over at Daniel, who was pulling at his collar and trying to read the program in the dark.

Daniel leaned in and whispered in my ear. The whole right side of my body got goose bumps. "So clue me in . . . what's the story on *Swan Lake*?"

I leaned in to whisper in his ear. My lips were dangerously close to his face. "She's a princess who's been cursed to live as a swan. He's hunting the swan but doesn't realize it's really the love of his life."

"Typical chick entertainment." Daniel snarled. "Lots of suffering and the guy is always wrong."

"It's a classic," I snapped. It was quiet for about two minutes, then he started up again.

"Now, see, if this was *Swan Lake 2: The Revenge*, Princess Buttercup down there would pull out some Jackie Chan moves and lay waste to the dude who cursed her. That's the ballet I want to see."

The woman next to me glared at us. "Shhh."

I slunk down in my seat, embarrassed. This was hopeless. He fidgeted. He took out a pencil and circled in all the Os in his program. By the end he was practically running for the exit doors.

As we headed outside, Daniel said, "If this is the

perfect girl's date, then I guess I'm going to be living alone the rest of my miserable life." He rocked back and forth on his heels cheerfully as I hailed a cab.

"It's not over yet," I said testily. I had the driver cut through the park and drive down to the Plaza hotel, where we could rent a horse and carriage by the hour. "Get in," I said. "Or do you have something against horses too?"

"Your wish is my command," he said, thumping his chest for effect. With the help of the driver we climbed into the backseat and set off for a ride through Central Park's gaslit streets. There was a slight breeze, and I was glad I'd worn Mom's sweater. The city seemed so quiet except for the clop–clop of the horse and the beating of my own heart.

"So what do you think?" I wasn't sure I wanted to know. I really wanted him to like it. To think I was cool for coming up with the horse ride.

"Not bad." Another carriage passed by, carrying a couple who were making out. Embarrassed, I looked away quickly. "So," I said, trying to get past the awkward moment. "I met your dad. What about your mom?"

Something shifted to dark in Daniel's eyes. He rubbed his hands over his knees and drummed his fingers. "My mom died."

"Oh, Daniel, I'm so sorry. What was she like?" I felt like I was really putting my foot in it. "I'm sorry. You totally don't have to answer that if you don't want to."

We drove under a tree. A low-lying branch tickled the tops of our heads. Daniel stretched out his hand and pulled down one leaf. He sat twirling it in his hand, watching it spin and blur like a ballerina. "Sometimes I forget, and then, you know, there'll be little things like a guy with a dancing chimp on TV or a lost-pet poster for some dog named Bubbles or something. And for a split second I want to show her, tell about it. I expect to see her looking at that lost poodle, giving it the thumbs-up and saying, 'Run, Bubbles, run, and don't look back, buddy. I'd run too if somebody named me Bubbles.' And then I remember that she's gone. It's like part of me just hollows out inside, and I can't fill it up again." Daniel turned his head and let the leaf blow out of his hand. "Ooh, the teen-angst portion of our program, folks."

He gave a little laugh, but he didn't turn back and look at me. I put my hand over his and held it. It was the same impulse that made me want to give advice to girls in a magazine and keep my mom from making a mistake with her life. He gave my hand a little squeeze, and we rode like that past Tavern on the Green, where happy people were spilling out of the famous restaurant, totally oblivious to broken hearts, lost chances, leaves blowing behind carriages in the wind.

The driver steered around by the zoo on the road back to the Plaza. "It's been really hard on my dad," he said after a while. "He was never exactly a barrel of laughs, but he really loved her. She lightened him up. Now he just throws himself into cause after cause and waits for me to do something he can be proud of, like be the only high-school junior to win the Pulitzer Prize."

"But you're the smartest person I know. How could he not be proud of you?"

Daniel gave me a funny look and a half smile. My stomach was doing total flip-flops. In the distance the lights of the Plaza winked at us. I willed the horse to slow down, to keep this night going. He hadn't let go of my hand yet, and now he seemed to realize it. Would he kiss me again? Could I manage not to screw it up if he did?

I didn't get a chance to find out.

"Okay, kids, end of the ride," the driver announced.

Daniel let go of my hand. "All I can say, DeWitt, is you better be ready for guy's-date night."

The moment, if there had been one, was over. We walked to the subway station. "Just show up tomorrow afternoon looking surly for Operation Derail. Okay?"

"Later," Daniel replied. I watched him slide his hand along the handrail down into the subway's depths. All I could think was, *He held my hand and didn't let go till he had to.*

Daniel

"You're here to see who?"

Lindsay's housekeeper, Consuela, was looking

me up and down like I was tainted fish in an outdoor market.

"Lindsay DeWitt? I'm Daniel Newman. She's expecting me." I tried to seem harmless. Consuela wasn't buying. She closed the door, and I started to wonder if this was all some practical joke of the Debonator's. I'd come as requested—tattered jeans, sneaks, scruffy hair, and the much desired Eat the Rich T-shirt. No wonder the housekeeper thought I was a door-to-door terrorist. Fortunately Lindsay came to save me.

"Hey. You look great," she said, all smiles. Man, that smile. It did things to me. I was trying to play it cool, though. I was still feeling a little weird about the night before and everything I'd said about my mom. I hadn't talked to anybody about her in so long. Not even Hakeem.

"Yeah. I'm at my best when I'm asked to come as a bum." I shrugged. Lindsay took my hand and pulled me into her house. The word *whoa* came to mind. You could've fit our entire dinky East Village apartment in their entry hall. Lindsay dropped my hand and asked me to follow her. Part of me wanted to keep holding hands. Another part of me wanted to run screaming into the street.

"This is some spread, DeWitt. Where's the pole that leads to the Bat Cave?"

"Wow, that was almost funny, Newman. You're improving."

"So, where's the easily offended future stepdad?" We'd taken a side trip into the humongous kitchen, where Consuela was alternately stuffing a chicken and giving me dirty looks. Lindsay motioned me over to a corner by a pantry, where she grabbed us some snack grub and sodas.

"I am so cursed," she whispered. "Jeffrey is held up in a meeting in Connecticut. He won't be back till tonight. And Mom decided spur of the moment to do some shopping. Now I'm stuck here with Alison and Marlon. Sorry. It's sort of a bust."

I twisted the top off my Coke and took a big swig. "Should we put the hoodoo on Alison? If we start acting radical, maybe she'll tell her dad marrying into your family is a bogus deal. Daddy does seem to dote on her every move."

Lindsay's brown eyes grew twinkly. "Plan B. I like it. Let's move."

Alison and Marlon were in the living room, watching E! and reading fashion magazines at the same time. Nice to know they could multitask. At first something seemed really strange about Alison. It finally dawned on me that she didn't have a cell phone attached to her ear.

"Alison. Marlon. You remember Dan, don't you?"

Marlon was totally engrossed in one of those ads for a drawing school at the back of a magazine. He was diligently trying to copy a picture of a sad clown. It wasn't pretty.

"Hi," Alison said, without looking up. "Oh my God. I can't believe there's a write-up on Prague in here. Now we'll never be able to go there again. It will be swarming with people from, like, Jersey and Brooklyn."

I was confused. "Prague? Isn't that a city? I mean, correct me if I'm wrong, but if you have a passport and the airfare, you're free to go, right?"

Alison gave me a condescending smile. "I'm talking about Prague, the restaurant? Down in Tribeca? Never mind."

I took that as my cue to plunge into plan B. "Yeah . . . well, well, well . . . I think I'll tell all my communist, antifashion friends to start hanging out there and bring down the cache value." I couldn't have been lamer if I'd said I didn't believe in the tooth fairy.

Lindsay shook her head. Then she got a mischievous gleam. "Daniel, is it true that you're doing research on big companies that are rumored to be laying off employees?"

"Yeah. In fact, right now I'm looking into Forrester Electronics." Actually my dad had given me that tidbit without even realizing it. This morning he'd muttered over Cocoa Puffs about the downsizing at the communications giant. "I hear your dad's gonna fire all the workers and hire cheap labor from Mexico." I studied Alison for a response. She didn't flinch.

"So what if he does?" she said.

I was going to have to kick into high gear. I went on and on about the evils of capitalism. I said it was a shame about that shoplifting habit of Lindsay's mom's and wondered aloud if anybody had found the pictures from that time she danced on a table wearing a shopping bag.

Finally Alison said more than three words. She fixed Lindsay with a steely stare.

"You know what I'm going to do?" We waited for her answer: *I'm going to tell my father to run like the wind because you're all crazy.* "I'm going to give you a makeover, Lindsay. Where's your room?"

I actually felt sorry for DeWitt. She looked like a puppy getting dragged to obedience school. Alison kissed Marlon on the cheek. "Back in a few, babe. Don't work too hard, okay?"

"I've almost go' it." Marlon was putting the finishing touches on his precious clown. Alison grabbed her huge purse and pulled Lindsay along behind her up the stairs like a little girl. She practically whimpered at me. I was about to laugh till I realized I was going to have to kill some time with the human negative-IQ man.

Marlon picked up a handful of popcorn and tried to toss it into his mouth without missing. "I like your style, mate."

"Excuse me?"

"That obnoxious bit you was putting on before?" Marlon said. "Bleedin' brilliant, man. You're preparing for a school play, are you?" He gave me the thumbs-up.

I hadn't even convinced the squash brain I was dangerous. So much for plan B.

Eight

Lindsay

"**N**OW, CLOSE YOUR eyes so I can line along the lashes." Alison was playing makeup guru, trying to get me in touch with my inner girlie-girl. I closed my eyes and let her put goop on my lids. It felt like she was swabbing me with paint.

"You're not going to make me look like Bozo, are you?"

"Just relax. I have wanted to give you a makeover for sooo long."

"Gee, thanks."

"Well, it's true. You're a pretty girl, Lindsay. You just need to bring it out more. Now, open your mouth just slightly. This color will be so amazing on you." Part of me wanted to sulk about being told I needed a makeover. But the other part of me figured I could do a little work to help her see how wrong my mother and I were for her and her dad.

"Can I see?" I asked, planning to insist she make me over like Marilyn Manson. That should scare Alison.

"Not yet," she said. "So, what's the speed dial on you and Grunge Boy?"

It took me a minute to realize she meant Daniel. "What do you mean?"

"I mean, I still don't know if you two are an item or what."

"No. Not really."

"Good. He's a little mental." I liked mental. Mental was adorable and very crushworthy. Alison studied my face for a second. I couldn't tell whether she thought I had potential or I was hopeless. "You know," she said, examining her makeup brushes. "You're so lucky, Lindsay."

Funny. I didn't feel lucky. I felt like a girl trying to keep her mom from getting married while also trying to keep from falling for the wrong guy herself. I was a big mess.

"Why am I so lucky?"

"Because." She shrugged, but a crease appeared on her usually smooth forehead. "You're smart. Everybody expects you to do something great someday."

"They do?"

"Sure," she said. "Your mom totally gushes over you."

I wanted to ask her more, to pry every single

78

slobbery detail out of her. "Moms do that," I said, throwing it away.

"Even my dad thinks you're cool."

I felt a little guilty about plan B now that I knew Jeffrey liked me. "He's nuts about you, Alison."

"He gives me things. But I don't know if he thinks I can be something special. Everybody expects me to look perfect all the time. Set a certain style. That's my talent. Hold your head down a little so I can pluck this straggly eyebrow."

"Ouch!" I winced as she pulled a hair that felt like it was rooted to my brain stem.

"No pain, no beauty," Alison said a little too cheerily. She brushed some peach blush over my cheeks. "Seriously, I'd love to have your smarts. Like, you'll probably get into Harvard or Princeton or something. I will too. But only because my dad's money will get me in."

Call me crazy, but I was actually feeling sympathy for Alison the blond terror. I'd only thought about how much it bites to be a klutz in the beauty department. I'd never considered what it would be like to be so pretty that you never had to work for anything, so pretty that you never had to develop your own dreams.

Alison handed me a tissue. "Blot your lips, and then I'll put on some gloss."

I dutifully kissed the tissue and started fishing. "So, Alison, are you happy that your dad is marrying my mom? Does he seem totally in love to you?"

"Trust me. My dad wouldn't marry someone

without a prenup if he wasn't nuts for her. I mean, it helps that your mom is rich too." So much for the kinder, gentler Alison Forrester. "Of course, she'll have to start dressing a little more conservatively. And she'll need to be on the boards of some women's clubs that are important to my dad. Join his country club in the Hamptons. Also, she should probably quit that little day job at the TV station. It's kind of tacky."

I was getting really steamed. I knew Jeffrey was the wrong guy for my mom. And this proved it. I would find a way to stop this wedding if it meant I had to drool and convulse on the floor. "My mom's not going to change. She's her own person, you know."

Alison shrugged and slathered my lips with pinky goop. "She's changed before. With all her other husbands, I mean. At least this time she's getting a good deal."

"A good deal?" I screeched. The lip-gloss wand streaked up my cheek.

Alison sighed. "You have to hold still, okay? Let me fix that." I tried to keep calm while she smudged at my streaky cheek. "You know, Lindsay . . . I could help you out too. Fix you up with a major hottie. Someone rich from a good family. And smart too."

Wow. So nice to know you could be both rich and smart. "No thanks. I can find my own dates."

"Okay." Alison sighed again. "But you can't be serious about bringing that loser to the wedding. What will people think?"

How dare she rag on Daniel? I was just about to tell her I was running away with him to an organic wheat-germ farm when Alison told me I could look now.

I checked out my reflection in the mirror. I had on more makeup than I'd ever worn in my life. I looked like . . . Alison. I looked . . . different, a little wilder. Not the same old boring *me*.

"Come on," she said, pulling me downstairs. Daniel's eyes got wide when I entered the living room. I took it as a good sign. I waited for him to say I was a goddess or at least that I was reasonably attractive. The silence was killing me.

"Well," I said, turning around. "What do you think?"

"Lindsay? Is that you? Hold on—you've been buried under a couple of tons of mascara."

I was not amused, but Marlon was. "That's genius! Buried under mascara—I like that one." He laughed.

"I think she looks fabulous," Alison said. "Lindsay, why don't you come out with us tonight? We're going to a fab restaurant. I know some guys who would die to meet you. You can wear something of mine."

"She can't," Daniel said. "She's coming to my house for a meeting of the Young Senseless Radical Society. We're planning to commit senseless acts of radicalness all over the city just as soon as we can stop being senseless long enough to plan them."

I knew he was trying to keep up with plan B.

81

But my heart wasn't in it right then. "Sorry," I told him. "I have plans with my mom. I really should get some writing time in before then. Daniel, thanks for coming by."

He gave me a funny look. "Sure."

I walked him to the door. "So I'll see you at *Blink* tomorrow." I pretended nothing was wrong, even though he'd really hurt my feelings. I couldn't wait to scrub my face and put on my slippers.

"Okay." He stopped on the front step. "Are you mad at me?"

"No," I lied. "Why would I be mad at you?"

"Right," he said uncertainly. "See you tomorrow."

I ran upstairs and washed my face till it was squeaky clean and a little red. So much for the glamour-girl approach. Alison and Marlon finally left, and Mom came home around eight-thirty. I was in the kitchen, indulging in a bowl of Ben & Jerry's butter-pecan ice cream.

"Yummy. Can I have a bite?" Mom didn't wait for an answer but dove in with a spoon like a vulture.

"No fair," I said, pulling the bowl away.

"You're right," she said through a mouthful of ice cream. "Besides, I have to fit in my wedding dress. Or maybe I could marry Ben and Jerry."

"Mom," I said, pushing the dregs in my bowl toward her waiting spoon. I knew she couldn't resist butter pecan. "Why did you and Daddy break up?"

Mom got that look that told me she wanted to spare me any pain. "Oh, honey. So many reasons. We were just kids ourselves, you know. And your father . . . well, he wasn't really ready for all the responsibility, I guess."

She reached out and patted my arm like she did when I was afraid to go to kindergarten. I let her hand stay. "Does Daddy love me?"

Mom scooted her chair next to mine and gave me a big, tight squeeze. "He loves you, Lindsay. I know he does. He's just got . . . limitations. You expect so much from people because you give a lot of yourself. But not everybody can love back the way you do."

"He doesn't have any trouble giving to Miles," I said, blinking away tears.

Mom pulled my head onto her shoulder and held me close. "I'm sorry, Linds. Really I am."

It wasn't the answer I wanted, but I knew it was the truth. My dad could only give me so much, and that wasn't enough. I didn't want to lose my mom too. "Mom? Maybe you should postpone the wedding."

Mom pulled back and gave me a raised eyebrow. "Why?"

"You don't even know this guy. I mean, he could have twelve wives all over the globe. He could be a creep."

Mom took another bite of my ice cream. "I promise—no other wives. I think I finally found my Prince Charming."

"What if he changes you, and you become just like all his snobby friends?" I was on the verge of sounding hysterical, but I couldn't stop myself.

Mom took the bowl, put it in the sink, and rinsed it out. "Linds, I don't know what this is about, but I am going to marry Jeffrey, and we are going to be a family. Why can't you be happy for me? It's been a long time since I've felt this way about someone."

I stared up at the ceiling to keep big, fat tears from spilling down my face. "I don't know. I just can't."

Mom put the bowl in the dishwasher and scrubbed at an imaginary spot on the immaculate kitchen countertop. "I saw that *An American in Paris* is coming on the ten o'clock movie. Do you want to get in our jammies and watch in my bed?"

"Sure," I whispered. "I'll be up in a minute."

"Okay," Mom said. I heard her heels clacking down the hall and up the stairs while I wondered whether I could possibly feel more alone.

Daniel

"Daniel, do you think you could be a panelist for our 'Fashion: Use It or Lose It' layout?"

Jen was badgering me to give phony guy commentary on girls' fashion choices. As if guys really cared whether a girl wore the latest shoes. Personally, I never understood the concept of high heels—like crippling yourself and not being able to walk faster than a snail is somehow sexy. I didn't get it. One of the editors broke in with a suggestion on a beauty special, and I pretended to be very interested. The real deal was that I was trying to figure out what was up with Lindsay. She'd been pretty cold to me ever since I'd dissed on her makeover. She'd ended up looking like Bride of Franken-Alison in all that goo. It so wasn't her.

I tried to make eye contact with her, but she was sitting at the other end of the table, doing her best to ignore me. I contemplated the spit-wad approach, but that seemed a little fourth grade. Also, Ann asked me a question and I was totally busted since I hadn't been paying attention to anything going on in the editorial meeting.

"I'm sorry. Could you repeat that?" I said, rustling papers to cover for the lack-of-hearing part.

Ann smirked. Unlike DeWitt, Ann made for a grade-A smirker. "Yes, Mr. Newman. If you care to join us, I was just asking what you thought about Greg's idea?"

"Greg's idea?" I repeated numbly.

"About a contest where someone who writes in to 'Girl's/Guy's View' could win a makeover?" Ann said it slowly and evenly.

"Oh, right." I glanced down at Lindsay, who was staring at a spot above my head somewhere. Makeovers. What was it with girls and wanting to change everything about themselves that guys liked in the first place? "I don't get the makeover thing."

"How so?" Ann said. For the first time all morning I had Lindsay's attention.

"Well, why can't girls just leave well enough alone? Quit messing with themselves all the time. Most guys like girls the way they are without all that extra . . . stuff." I saw Lindsay's mouth pull into a shy smile. She had really nice lips. *Focus, Newman. Focus.*

Ann drummed her fingers on the table and nodded like she'd just answered an internal question for herself. "That's very insightful, Daniel. Maybe you could write a special opinion piece about this topic."

"I could call it 'Ten Annoying Things Girls Do to Turn Guys Off.'"

That got the Debonator up and talking. "We'd need a whole special issue to cover the annoying things guys do."

"All right, settle down," Ann said.

"I'd love to have a front-row seat inside a guy's head," Jen gushed. I could smell a new assignment coming my way.

"How about it, Daniel? Can you give us a list of guy turnoffs and turn-ons?" Ann fixed me with her businesslike stare.

"Sure, whatever," I said. Lindsay shook her head in disbelief. I couldn't wait to put this list together. While Ann went over story ideas with the staff, I scribbled down my innermost thoughts on all things girl related.

A Guy's View:
Big-Time Girl Turn-ons
and Serious Turnoffs.

Turn-on
Girls who play an instrument.
Turnoff
Girls who use guys like instruments.

Turn-on
Brainpower. A girl who knows current events, music, sports, etc.
Turnoff
Brain drains. A girl who wouldn't know the president's cabinet from a kitchen cabinet.

Turn-on
Girls who know how to laugh—even at themselves.
Turnoff
Girls who take themselves way too seriously.

Turn-on
Girls with a natural, easy style.
Turnoff
Girls whose style takes three hours to put on.

I could have probably made a list three miles long, but Ann called the meeting to a halt. Lindsay gathered up her stuff and was out of her seat so fast, I could barely catch up. She brushed past me on her way out of the conference room. I grabbed her arm. "So are you going to ignore me for the rest of my life? Or can I say sorry and get back in the land of the living?"

Lindsay punched my arm playfully. "Sorry. Guess I was feeling a little sensitive yesterday."

"Yeeeahhh. Just a little. Speaking of sensitive, as in sensitive, wonderful guys, you still haven't gone out on my perfect date yet. How about next Saturday? You busy?"

"It had better not involve sports," Lindsay said.

"Hey, you made me go to the ballet. As far as I'm concerned, I could take you to see monster-truck races and it would still not be as torturous as what you put me through."

"Okay, okay. Oh, and I've been thinking about plan B," Lindsay said. "How would you like to use those *Time* magazine skills of yours to dig up stuff on Jeffrey?"

"You want me to spy on Jeffrey?"

"No. I just want you to find out if he's an okay guy. And if he's not, I want to know about it."

"I don't know. Seems kind of harsh, checking out your about-to-be stepdad."

"Look, if he's a good guy, I will never say another word. I just don't want my mom to get hurt. Will you do it for me? Please?"

"Okay, I'll do it. Now scram. I have research to do."

I hit the Internet. I had to admit that the prospect of getting a real scoop on somebody like Jeffrey Forrester was pretty tempting. With one story I could write my own ticket into a great journalism school and maybe even a job at *Newsweek*. Something about Lindsay wanting to watch out for her mom hit at me too.

I flashed back to my mom. She was wearing her pink bathrobe. It was the bad days, toward the end, when she couldn't get out of bed. I was rubbing her feet. She would smile and say, "Oh, rapture," in this whispery, fake British voice. Oh, rapture. She thought it was a hassle for me to rub her feet. I would have rubbed her feet till my hands fell off if I thought it would keep her here in her pink bathrobe with her funny voices and warm smiles forever. Lindsay was just looking out for her mom. What kind of guy wouldn't help out?

Every search engine led to a gazillion pieces on Forrester. My eyes crossed and recrossed reading boring page after page about his life: personal wealth, building an empire, first marriage, Alison, his divorce, charitable contributions. Nothing interesting. I didn't know whether to feel relieved for Lindsay's sake that I hadn't uncovered anything on Jeffrey or disappointed for my sake that my big scoop was a total bust.

Hey, wait a minute. What was this? I scrolled down the article, buried in a very old piece about new millionaires. I read as fast I could. The gist was that he made a contribution to a judge in Mississippi every year. Now, why would he do that? Call me Scoop Newman, but it smelled like a cover-up to me.

"Why in Mississippi?" I wondered out loud. Forrester was from Connecticut.

And why was I so happy that I'd done good by Lindsay?

Nine

Daniel

Ten Reasons I Need to Stop Thinking
About Lindsay DeWitt

1. *We work for the same magazine, and it's totally un-professional.*
2. *She dates guys named Tanner and Remington and other non-first-name first names.*
3. *Her mom is marrying one of the country's richest dudes.*
4. *I have to write a profile of her and Alison. See reason number one above.*
5. *I haven't even started said profile and don't want to.*

I only made it to number five before an image of Lindsay made me smile all the way to my socks. The fact was, I was starting to look forward to hanging with Lindsay. I liked helping her on her crazy mission to get the 411 on Jeffrey. And it was pretty exciting to think that I, Daniel B. Newman, might actually file a real and important story. (The B. stands for Benjamin, by the way.)

Just thinking about my name as a byline under an AP story had me psyched. I could see it all playing out: *Genius Teen Reporter Busts Jeffrey Forrester; Newman First on Scene with Story, see related story, Supermodels Arrested in Pajama Party Spree with Teen Reporter, page 19*. Oh yeah. This would play. And maybe for once my dad would come alive again.

The logical person to squeeze info from was Alison. Since she'd made the mistake of giving me her cell-phone number during our day out, I figured I'd be able to catch her without too much trouble. Hopefully she'd buy my excuse about needing more Alison, capital *A,* for the pages of *Blink*. She answered after only two rings. I could hear hair-dryer noises in the background.

"Hi, Alison. It's Daniel Newman. I . . . where are you?"

"Having a pedicure," she shouted. "Hold on— Svetlana, that one's too purple. Let's go more pinky-brown. What's up?"

Cool. Be cool, Newman. "Nada. Just wanted a little more about you for the profile. I was doing this whole family-history angle, and I came across a name I didn't know. A judge. Leonard Bastrop? Ring a bell?"

"Uncle Lenny?"

Bingo! "He's your uncle?"

"Well, not really. He's some old friend of

Daddy's, and I mean old. Like he's practically falling over. Daddy told me to call him Uncle Lenny. Ooh, I like that, Svetlana. Maple Frost. Delish."

I wasn't sure where to go with the questions. I was hoping for more. "So, like, he comes over to visit a lot and stuff."

"No. Not really. He lives in Mississippi, so we don't see him too often. Why do you want to know?"

"Oh, no reason," I lied. "Listen, it sounds like you're pretty busy there. I don't want to hold you up."

"Uncle" Lenny. Sounded pretty suspicious to me. Alison hung up at the exact moment my dad peeked his head in my bedroom door, followed by his six-foot-four body. Did the guy ever hear of knocking?

"I was thinking of ordering Chinese for dinner," my dad said. "You hungry?"

"I could go for Chinese. Can we get fried dumplings?"

"Steamed is healthier."

"Yeah, but I'm only sixteen. I've got another forty years before I have to bargain with my food. Fried. And an egg roll."

Dad sort of smiled. "Egg roll and hot mustard. Sounds good."

It was nice to see him attempting to joke around, even if it was only about Chinese food. "So . . . Dad. I kind of need to ask a favor."

"The answer is no. What's the question?" This

time he really did smile. Like I saw bits of teeth and everything.

I felt embarrassed about asking for money, but my *Blink* paycheck was pretty pathetic, and I wasn't even getting it till after the "perfect guy's date." I shoved my hands in my pockets. "Well, I'm taking this girl out on this, I don't know, sort of a date."

Dad nodded. "Sort of a date. Good, good. Wouldn't want you to just go on a date date."

My face was flushed. I know it sounds totally Hallmark, but I was so happy to see my dad again—my dad the way I remembered him before Mom died. Joking around. "I've got tickets to see the Rangers at the Garden, but I'm a little light in the cash department. Interested in giving to a good cause?"

Dad reached into his wallet and pulled out a ten. I stared at it. "Uh, Dad? Hello? It's no longer the seventies. I couldn't go to McDonald's on ten bucks. Sorry, dude."

"Capitalist youth. That's what's wrong with this country." He pulled out a twenty and took back the ten. Cheap was my dad's middle name, but at least I could spring for hot dogs.

"Thanks," I said, pocketing the money fast.

"So who's the girl?"

The moment of truth could wait. "No one you know. She's pretty cool. She reminds me a little bit of . . ." I stopped like someone had dropped cold water over my head, but it was too late. Dad's pained look came back. I had almost mentioned the

M word. Lindsay did remind me of Mom in some ways. They were both so completely honest. It was the first time I'd made the connection.

"Well, have a good time," Dad said, and headed for the door. I couldn't let him leave like that.

"Dad . . ." I trailed off. Something the size of Nebraska caught in my throat, and my chest grew heavy. "I just miss her, y'know?"

Dad kept his hand on the door and his face to the wall like he was studying my light switch. "You can't bring her back, son."

A million pins seemed to be pricking at my eyes. My voice got quavery. "I know that. It's just . . . why can't we talk about her? She wasn't a storm that was here and gone, you know. I wish . . ." I lay back and hugged the pillow to my chest, trying to push the sobs back inside.

Dad sat on the edge of the bed, his back to me, his hand on my shoe. He sounded far away and lost. "Sometimes when I first wake up in the morning, before I'm really awake, I think, oh, Suzanna's in the shower, and we'll take the train in to work together. I think everything is normal again. And then the room gets a little clearer, the bed a little bigger, and I remember that she's gone. I have to tell myself that she's gone. I can't let myself remember or the pain . . . I'm sorry, Daniel. I just can't, buddy."

Dad made no noise when he cried. His big shoulders moved up and down like a machine. I was so fascinated watching him that I forgot to cry.

After a few minutes it was over. The storm had passed, and the air felt all sticky. The weight of tears.

Dad blew his nose on the handkerchief he always keeps in his pants pocket. "I was thinking maybe sesame chicken to go with the dumplings and egg roll."

"Yeah. Sounds good," I said. My voice was hollow.

"Okay, then. I'll go order."

"I'll be down in a few."

Dad closed the door behind him, and I was alone again.

Lindsay

"So, Caroline, everyone's *dying* to know the dish on your wedding. We're *thrilled* that you're here with your lovely daughter, Lindsay, and future stepdaughter, Alison."

Shoot me. That's what I was thinking as Mom, Alison, and I sat on live TV at her station, being interviewed by the world's worst gossip reporter, Melanie Moore. She was the type who used lots of adjectives. You could practically feel the words being underlined, bolded, and capped in the air. The station was milking the mom-wedding-of-the-century thing to the hilt. They'd even created a little countdown logo and a man-on-the-street segment that they did every day. Today Melanie had us on her show to talk about all the girlie stuff like dresses and makeup and everything. Again I say, Shoot me.

Mom smiled as brightly as the studio lights that were making me feel a little sweaty. "Oh, Melanie, you know I'd give you good dish. Don't I always?"

Mom and Melanie laughed like they were best friends. It was making me want to gag. I had never noticed Mom being so phony before. I was sure it was Jeffrey's influence. Alison, of course, loved being on TV.

"I love the way you're wearing your hair now," she said, fawning all over Melanie.

"Oh," Melanie said, patting an upswept hairdo that was the size of a Cadillac. "Thank you, honey. So, Alison, tell me about that *dashing* boyfriend of yours, Marlon Cassidy. Is he a hunk or what, people?" Melanie held up a picture of Marlon looking surly on the cover of GQ. He seemed so chiseled and threatening—not at all the sort of lovable idiot he was in real life.

Alison put her hand to her face and pretended to be embarrassed. Like the day that Alison blushes for real will be the day the world stops turning on its axis. "Yeah, he is so good-looking. I guess I'm a pretty lucky girl."

Melanie patted her knee in a grandmotherly way. "I think he must be lucky to have such a *gorgeous* girlfriend as you, honey. Is this girl not *stunning?* I could die to look like that. Please."

Alison did her patented gracious I'm-really-very-shy look. "That's very sweet of you to say,

Melanie. I'm just glad to be here today to talk about something really special we're doing after the wedding. As you know, I'm on the board for a charity, Homeless Dogs Need You."

She had to be kidding. The only charity I could imagine Alison being a part of was something that gave old Prada shoes to impoverished teens around the nation. Melanie was lapping it up like chocolate. She put on her serious, concerned face.

"Yes, tell us about your idea, Alison."

"Well, I'm going to auction off my bridesmaid dress after the wedding to raise money for the dogs. I mean, I'll never wear it again, and it could do so much good for these poor animals that are abandoned."

"That is so sweet. What a *wonderful* idea, Alison. Caroline, you must be so proud to have such a sweetie in your family."

Mom beamed. "Yes. Alison is a special girl. She's teaching me a lot about opening your heart."

Opening your heart? To what? The Barney's one-day sale? The love fest was really activating my hurl reflex. I took a sip of water and spilled some on my blouse. Great. Now I had a big wet spot on the top of my boob. I crossed my arms and tried to look natural. Melanie finally seemed to notice I was there.

"And Lindsay, what about you? Will you be auctioning off your gown for Alison's charity?"

Okay. You know that angel and devil that square off on your shoulders? Well, this time the devil on my shoulder gave the angel a boot to the floor. What if I were really horrible? Would Jeffrey be so mortified that he'd postpone the wedding? Would he insist that Mom send me to military school and she'd angrily tell him that she'd choose me over him? Melanie was staring at me, waiting for me to be just like the Alisons of the world. She could keep waiting.

"Actually, I'm auctioning off my dress to support the Communist Party."

Melanie was still smiling like I'd said I liked daffodils and old movies on AMC. "The what, dear?"

"The communists. I've been dating this guy, he's a communist radical, and he has opened my eyes—as well as my heart—to how much money we waste. It's really criminal."

I could feel Mom's eyes burning a hole through my left side. She laughed, but I could tell it wasn't a real one. "Lindsay is our resident jokester. She's always coming up with crazy stuff to make us laugh. Lindsay, honey, why don't you tell Melanie all about your dresses? Vera Wang did them for us. The girls look so beautiful."

"I'm *dying* to see them. I bet that cost a pretty penny. . . ." Melanie looked meaningfully at Mom, who was acting coy.

"Actually," I blurted out, "the dresses are pink, as are the shoes. I'm thinking of dying my hair pink to match. I mean, if you're going to come to a wedding dressed as a grapefruit, might as well go all the way. Right?"

I actually heard a producer gasp. I knew Mom was going to kill me, but I hoped she'd have a chance to see Jeffrey for what he was—shallow and social climbing.

"Whatever," Alison said. "I'm sure Price would just love to see you in pink hair. Not."

"I'm not going with Price. I'm taking Daniel."

"That slob reporter? Please. Does he even know how to dress for a formal event?"

"Sure. His dress is pink too."

Melanie had been watching Alison and me volley back and forth like a spectator at the U.S. Open. Now she jumped in. "What's his name, Lindsay, dear?"

"Daniel. Daniel Newman."

"His father isn't well-known ACLU attorney Robert Newman, is he?"

I hadn't thought about how far this could go. Now I was stuck. "Yes," I said in a small voice. "He is."

"My. Looks like you're going to have your hands full, Caroline. Well, this is certainly a *lively* discussion. Sounds like this wedding will be even more interesting than we thought. That's all the time we have for today. Thanks for stopping by, ladies."

Mom didn't speak to me till we were safely in a taxi on the way home. "Are you going to tell me what that was all about?"

I felt like a five-year-old who just drew on the walls with crayons. I needed to keep my cool. "You never would've done all this air-kiss stuff before you got engaged to Jeffrey." You could hear the pout in my voice. So much for keeping my cool.

"It has nothing to do with Jeffrey. It has to do

with you embarrassing me on TV. The papers should have a field day with this."

"Is that all you care about now? The press coverage?" I was really being mean, but I couldn't seem to stop myself.

"That was unfair, and you know it."

She was right. I did know it. I was starting to see things in my mom I didn't like. Had they always been there? Or was it Jeffrey? It had to be Jeffrey. "You never spend time with me anymore. You're always off with Jeffrey. You haven't even involved me in any of the wedding preparations."

Mom let out a long sigh. "Honey, there's a lot to do right now—a lot to take care of for the wedding. I'm sorry that I've been so busy. But you're not acting like yourself. Is this that boy's influence? That Daniel Newman—the communist's son?"

Oops. Now I understood how rumors get started, only I had set this one in motion. "Can we just leave him out of this?"

"Seems to me that you're the one who brought him in, Lindsay."

I leaned my head back against the seat. How had I made such a mess of things in less than thirty minutes? What was the phrase—"Oh, what a tangled web we weave, when first we practice to deceive"? And I was neck deep in the tanglies.

We rode a good ten blocks in traffic, neither one of us saying a word. It was awful. I felt like the world's most rotten daughter. And at the same time my mom seemed alien to me. A pod person with a great wardrobe and a perfect smile who was about to marry the wrong guy and plunge me into a life I so did not want—a life where I couldn't get away from Alison Forrester. My plan was backfiring big time. I needed something to break the ice with Mom and pull us out of the cold war.

"I spy with my little eye . . . something that starts with the letter *A*."

"An apology, perhaps?" Okay. So Mom wasn't in game mood. Ouch. A minute later she looked out her window. "Is it apples?"

I saw the fruit cart on the sidewalk with its shiny, waxed apples nestled next to bananas and grapes. "Nope," I said. "Try again." My mom never could resist this game. She always had to know the answer.

"Hmmm, is it Angela's Diner?" She pointed to the blue-and-white sign hanging above a restaurant where an old man was drinking his coffee at a table in the large window.

"Got it."

"Can't stump me for long. My turn. I spy with my little eye . . . a mopey girl."

"You have to give the letter, not the object. And I'm not moping," I said, in full mope.

"Honey, on the level, are you upset that it's not just going to be you and me, the dynamic duo, anymore?"

She thought I was jealous of Jeffrey? Was I jealous of Jeffrey? Okay, maybe I was. A little. I liked having Mom to myself. But it was more than that. I totally thought Mom was making a mistake—one that could really hurt her. Embarrass her. Like I'd just embarrassed her on TV.

Oh, boy. Suddenly life was getting very messy.

"Mom, can't you just wait to marry Jeffrey? Make it a Christmas wedding? You know how you love Christmas, and I'll come dressed as a snowman!"

Mom let out another one of those patented elegant sighs. "Lindsay, I am marrying Jeffrey on July 29. And you will be there in a pink dress and normal hair, and that is that. Do you understand me?"

"Jawohl," I snapped. We were stopped at a light just a few blocks from *Blink*'s offices. I jumped out of the cab in a huff.

"Lindsay! Where do you think you're going, young lady!"

Young lady? She hadn't called me that since my preschool days. I kept walking, my 'tude fueling each stride. I called back over my shoulder, "I wouldn't want you to be seen with me. Might be too embarrassing for you."

I knew I'd pay for that comment later. But it felt good to get all spin-on-your-heels. Fine. Let her marry Jeffrey and ruin our lives. See if I cared. I'd move to France and join a mime troupe. As I plotted my great escape, I bumped into Daniel a block from *Blink*.

"Hey, where's the fire?"

"My mom will be roasting me over it later, I think."

"Whoa. What did you do? Use the wrong salad fork at lunch?"

"Ha ha. Very funny." An uncomfortable pinch grabbed at my heart as I remembered mentioning Daniel's name on TV. Should I confess? Tell him I'd told a bit of a tall tale on him? Maybe I'd get lucky and it would all blow over. And maybe I'd be the next Michael Jordan. "It's nothing," I said, my cheeks blushing anyway. "Just wedding stuff."

Daniel leaned against the side of the building, letting his backpack rest on a trash can. In the sun his blond hair was a halo. He was wearing those plastic Mardi Gras beads they sell at concerts. It forced me to look at his kissable, light brown neck, hovering dangerously close. I looked away from his neck at his face. He was a golden boy with a golden smile. A smile that could get a girl to hop a freight train or sky dive into the Grand Canyon.

"Listen," he said. "I think I'm on to something about Forrester. I'm following up on it. It's pretty cool, working on a real story. Thanks, DeWitt." He kicked at my shoe. I kicked back. "Oh. Don't forget about our date on Saturday."

Forget? I was living for it. "Oh . . . is that this Saturday?"

"You're such a bad liar, DeWitt. Should I pick you up or—"

"I'll meet you," I snapped. My mom would go ballistic if she crossed paths with him right now.

"Okay. I'll be in front of Madison Square Garden under the big sign. Six-thirty. Do not be late, or some goons will steal our seats."

"Gee, that would be a tragedy."

Daniel sauntered down the steps. "If you don't want to stand for two and a half hours, it would be."

My in box was filled with lonely hearts. Daniel had just posted his "Guy's View" on a few of them.

I read—and disagreed—with all of his responses. But one really caught my eye.

> Dear Girl's/Guy's View:
>
> I'm serious as a heart attack—I've got it bad for this adorable guy, but he's all sweaty palmed over this "perfect" girl. She couldn't be more different from me, and I wonder if I'm his type. Should I kiss him off or hang in there and hope he figures out that I'm really his dream girl?
>
> Confused in Queens, NY

Daniel's response had me seeing red:

> Dear Confused,
>
> Here's the thing: Does the "perfect" girl like him back? Maybe he's hung up on her because she doesn't know he's alive. (Guys do this. We like to torture ourselves. I don't make the rules of guydom—I just follow 'em.) Or maybe he doesn't know you like him. If you get the feeling he's mooning over this girl, but it's just not gonna happen for them, I say wait till it blows over, then let the guy know how you feel about him. But the real word is this: Don't sit around pining for him. Get out there and have a life. If it's meant to be, then great. If not, you haven't wasted any time. And that's a Guy's View of it.

Could he be any more misguided? I had to save that girl in Queens from having any hope that this guy would fall for her instead of Miss Perfect Thang.

Dear Confused,

As usual, if you want good love advice, you have to get it from your own kind. You should run, don't walk, away from this guy and his hang-up on Perfect Girl. Even if she is totally wrong for him, he'll follow her till she goes out with him and they'll end up in some tortured Dawson's Creek *triangle that you'll have to hear about every time they break up—which will be every other Friday. Do yourself a favor and give up on him now. This is the Girl's View, and believe me, it's the right one.*

There. Now she knew the score. There was no point in wondering whether a guy was going to fall in love with a dream girl, like a Suki, instead of you. There was no point in spending time with him, going with him to Madison Square Garden, or thinking about him whenever your brain wasn't filled with the basics of survival like food and sleep. There was no point, but I knew that Confused in Queens would go on hoping anyway. Because that's the way the heart works. It just does.

Besides, I was giving advice that I couldn't follow myself. My heart worked that way too. And deep inside that strange little beating muscle, I wanted to believe there was hope for me. I stared at the words on my screen and watched them disappear as I hit delete.

Ten

Daniel

I WAS THE one who was late. The trains were all screwed up, and I got to MSG at seven o'clock instead of six-thirty. Lindsay was waiting in front of the huge marquee, looking less than friendly. She was sweet and pretty in her jeans and button-down combo. Maybe her look was growing on me too.

"Do you like hot dogs?" I asked her.

"Doesn't everybody?"

We sort of jogged through the throngs of people, me pulling Lindsay behind me. We didn't really have much time, but I didn't want to cop to that and let her dog me about it all night long. We arrived at one of New York's greatest delicacies—a Nathan's hot-dog stand.

"Ta-da!" I held my arms open like a circus barker. Lindsay wrinkled her nose.

"Gee, really springing for the big bucks tonight,

Newman. Will we be able to sit for our luxury meal, or is it strictly a stand-and-gobble routine?"

"What are you talking about?" I said, desperately scanning the crammed space for two available stools. They did not materialize. "You gotta love Nathan's. It's an institution. And sitting ruins the whole mood of it."

Lindsay gave me the arched eyebrow. "There are no seats."

"Yeah, well, there's that too." I squeezed my way up to the counter and ordered three hot dogs (two for me), two fries, a lemonade, and a root beer. I was hoping the hot dog wouldn't leave me with you-know-what breath. I had ordered ours without onions and then felt totally embarrassed about it. Like I might as well just go ahead and say, "Big kiss coming later," if you know what I mean. But this wasn't that kind of date. This was a standing-up-for-mankind kind of date, even if the sight of Lindsay trying to laugh without spitting out her hot dog made my heart do a funny flip. Call me wacky. I like girls who eat with gusto.

"So I'm guessing that exhibition hockey game on the marquee is for real. No chance it will morph into the Ice Follies?" Lindsay took a big gulp of her lemonade.

"If it does, there is something seriously wrong with the coaching staff."

"How come they're playing hockey in the middle of the summer?"

"It's an exhibition game. Sort of an off-season

practice. If it was the real season, I would've had to sell you to get the tickets."

"Good to know my personal worth has climbed to the price of two hockey tickets."

Two guys loitering outside suddenly snapped off a couple of pics. "Hey, those guys just snapped a picture of us. Is there a Nathan's newsletter or something?"

Lindsay got this weird expression on her face. "Probably paparazzi. Ignore them."

"Why would they want our pictures?"

"It's nothing, okay? Just eat."

I looked up at the clock and about had a heart attack. "Whoa. It's getting late. You don't mind eating the rest of that on the fly, do you?"

I stuffed a few napkins in my pocket and pulled Lindsay toward Madison Square Garden. She dropped the remains of her fries in a Dumpster. "So much for a nice, relaxing meal."

Our seats were in the nosebleed section, but I didn't care. For some reason, it felt really right being at the Garden, watching hockey with Lindsay. I just felt completely at home. Lindsay wasn't really digging the big-guys-with-sticks-hitting-small-objects-across-the-ice thing, though.

Fortunately the game ended without going into overtime, or I think I would have had a mutiny on my hands. We poured out of the Garden with the rest of New York and waited for the F train to the East Village. I noticed the photographer dudes from Nathan's had staked us out on the subway platform, but I did my best to ignore them as I had been advised. Besides, I was pretty psyched about showing Lindsay my favorite hangout, The Coffeehouse. My rule was, if you liked The Coffeehouse, you were all right. If you didn't, we were just from two different worlds. I wondered where Lindsay and I would end up.

Fifteen minutes later we were stepping into the dark den. The tables all had big, fat candles on them. There were some guys onstage playing some funky-weird techno using computers and old synths.

"So, what do you think?" I asked nervously.

Lindsay took a look around and nodded. "It's as bizarre as you are, Newman. I like it."

Another big score for Daniel Newman.

"Hey, Newman!"

I turned around and was face-to-face with Hakeem and Jack, who blew me an air kiss. I was glad to see them but a little shy about introducing them to Lindsay. As usual, Hakeem poured on the charm.

"You must be Lindsay. *Bon soir,*" he said, giving a little half bow. "I'm Hakeem."

Jack grabbed Lindsay's hand and pumped it like he was running for office. "Jack."

Lindsay let loose with a real killer of a smile. I'm not kidding when I say her whole face lit up. "Hey, at least your friends have class, Newman. No telling what happened to you."

Hakeem and Jack were thrilled, of course. They

110

exchanged high fives with the Debonator and tortured me with the obvious fact that I had been dissed. I know it sounds goofy, but I was secretly jazzed that Lindsay had broken the ice with my best buds. I wanted them to like her and vice versa. It was getting weird.

Hakeem ushered us back to a table they had in the corner, and I used the last of my dad's twenty bucks to buy us a couple of lattes.

"So, the Dan Man is showing you the guy's version of a perfect date, eh?" Jack was grinning from ear to ear and rubbing his hands together in fiendish delight. "What's the verdict from the double-X-chromosome crowd?"

"Well," Lindsay said, stirring her latte. "I choked down a hot dog so I could sit for two hours on cold, hard seats and watch big, burly men attack each other with sticks. That doesn't say much for evolution."

Hakeem grabbed his heart in mock pain. "Oh, this one is harsh. No appreciation for the finer things in guy life."

"Yeah, I'm scared to see what's coming next."

What's coming next? What did she mean? "This is next," I said, a little defensively.

"Coffee and geeks making computer noise?"

"No. Hanging out with the guys."

Lindsay leaned back and crossed her arms over her chest. I knew that stance. It wasn't good. "And what do we do now that we're here?"

How could she manage to make one little

question sound so intimidating? Jack rushed in to answer. "We hang out. Shoot the breeze. Hang out some more. You know, it's a hang thing."

Hakeem nodded in agreement. We all knew this was the order of the universe.

"Oh, I see," Lindsay said in that sarcastic tone. "Wow, well, what girl wouldn't just die to sit in a coffee bar on a date with a guy and all his friends just hanging out? Sounds dreamy."

I was not letting that pass unchallenged. "Girls just hang out too. It's just that they're not content to call it that. No, they've gotta hound the guy to come up with two or three guy friends to set up with their girlfriends so they can all go out together because otherwise the girlfriends get mad. And then once they're all together on this date, the girls spend half the time running off to the bathroom so they can ditch the guys and talk about them."

"The man tells the truth," Hakeem said.

Lindsay's eyes got big. Big score. She laughed. "That is so not true."

Jack joined the conversation, but he was lagging behind by a few seconds. "Wow. How come nobody's ever asked me to hook up on that kind of date? Like, I'd be a good setup for somebody."

"You're getting off program, Jack. The point is, girls do stupid things, but they like to pretend that only guys do."

"At least I know how to plan a date instead of just using the lame hangout excuse."

Hakeem started laughing. "Oh, man, she got you there, bro."

Jack was fixating. "Seriously, dude, you've never called me to be, like, your backup on a group date. What's up with that?"

I needed to wrestle control. Prove that my way was the right way and her way was the silly girls' way. "You know what your problem is, DeWitt? You're not spontaneous."

Lindsay's eyes flashed. "Excuse me?"

The table got quiet. Even Jack had stopped being self-involved and was watching the show-down. "You heard me," I said, growing bolder. "You lack spontaneity. You need everything ordered and planned. There's no go with the flow."

"Oh, really?" She got this tone I didn't like. I had the feeling she was about to hop off the teeter-totter and let me drop. Without another word, she marched over to the jukebox (the technonerd brothers had thankfully stopped playing), dropped in two quarters, and punched in a few selections. Three seconds later the opening bars of Aretha Franklin's "Respect" filled the room. People instinctively started to bop their heads and catch the groove.

Lindsay made her way back to the table, but she didn't sit. Instead she climbed up on top and started to dance. She wasn't going to win a place in a video anytime soon, but she could sway okay. Then she started to sing along—if you could call it that. I've heard some bad singers in my time, and let me tell

113

you, Lindsay DeWitt has them all beat. Plus she was loud.

It was like a car accident. A train wreck. A car accident *and* a train wreck. It was also really fantastic. Some customers threw napkins. Others clapped and cheered. And the whole time Lindsay addressed her crazy table-dance number to my face. Burn.

A flashbulb went off. Then two more. The entire room was exploding. Holding a hand up to shield my eyes, I turned around and saw Laurel and Hardy, our shutterbug friends, snapping away at the whole spectacle. Somebody pushed them out the door. That's about the time management in the form of a Buddhist bouncer the size of a truck came over and peacefully threw us out. At least he was nice about it and just said we were "not in harmony with The Coffeehouse vibe."

"Hey, Lindsay!" One of the photographers started snapping again, and the other began walking toward us from his perch across the street.

"Why is that guy following us?" I asked.

"I guess I should have warned you. I was a little bit 'spontaneous' on TV the other day. I mentioned you were my date. Also that you were a known communist radical. Now, run."

Hakeem and Jack sprinted down the street toward Tompkins Square Park. "See you guys later!" Hakeem laughed. One of the photographers gave chase, but I didn't stick around to find out how it all ended. Lindsay and I bolted up St. Marks Place. We were in my neighborhood now, and if some out-of-shape, middle-aged paparazzi guy wanted to chase us, he'd have to be really good. He was. By the time we ran across the intersection at Second Avenue, he was gaining on us. I could see a bus pulling up to the stop at the corner of St. Marks and Third Avenue.

"Faster!" I screamed.

The bus doors were just about to close. I took a flying leap onto the steps of it, hauling Lindsay in behind me. "Go!" I shouted to the astonished bus driver, who immediately shut the doors and sailed off down Third Avenue. Outside on the street the photographer was bent over, cursing and trying to catch his breath.

Lindsay and I were alternately panting and laughing, the excitement of the whole chase having given us the giggles. The bus driver regained his composure long enough to bark that we'd better have the proper fare. I swiped twice with my MetroCard, and we grabbed two seats on the almost empty bus.

Night scrolled past our window, lit up by a thousand lights and dreams. "Where does this bus go?" I asked.

"I have no idea. It's feeling spontaneous too."

I didn't care where it took us. I wanted the night to go on forever, the road bumping along beneath us, the adrenaline slowing in our veins, and Lindsay as close as possible.

Lindsay

I giggled when I woke up the next morning. I actually rolled over and giggled about it all. It felt that good to be alive. My legs were sore from running pell-mell through the East Village next to Daniel. He'd even let me borrow his jacket to sneak into my house once we spotted the reporters across the street. I could still smell him on my arms. Okay, true confession? I slept in it. I didn't want to take it off and have the night end. Things were about as perfect as they could be until I heard my mom screeching my name from downstairs. Screeching is generally not a pleasant thing. Not anxious to meet my doom, I rolled over and put the pillow over my head.

Mom marched right into my room and snatched it off. Jeffrey was right behind her. They stood over me waving the *New York Post*. The front page showed a familiar girl dancing on a table and an adorable, bewildered-looking guy gaping at her from his chair. Oops.

Mom read the headline out loud and with feeling. "'DeWitt's Daughter Out of Control!' I don't know what's gotten into you lately," Mom fumed. "First the TV show, now this. Maybe we should send her to a spa for a couple of days till this whole thing dies down," she directed to Jeffrey. "And she could relax and get a makeover."

"Sure, babe. Whatever you want." Jeffrey was overjoyed to be able to say something.

I was stunned. I had expected Jeffrey to respond this way, not my mom. This was so not like her. "Why are you talking about me like I'm not even here?"

Mom softened from Helga the Horrible to Helga the Concerned Sitcom Mom. "Honey, do you need some time with Mom? We could go to that spa we talked about—the place your friend Jen recommended? The one that has the Japanese mud wraps?"

I knew she was trying, but I didn't want to be wrapped up in anything except Daniel. "No, Mom. I'm fine. Really."

Jeffrey perked up and sat on the bed next to Mom. With his stocky body and balding head, he reminded me of a big beetle I wanted to thwack out of existence. "I got it. You girls always like to get your hair done. Why don't you make a day of it on me? My treat."

He gave Mom a big hug, and she kissed him on the lips and looked at him adoringly. It was a little much for morning. Yecch. I waited for Mom to set him straight on what girls like. "That's a great idea, honey. Have I told you that you are the best?"

Double yecch. Jeffrey handed me his credit card like it was the passkey to heaven. "Here you go, toots." Yes, he called me toots. "Go anyplace you want. If they give you a hassle about getting in on short notice, you tell them to give me a call, okay?"

I stared at the platinum American Express in my hand. So Mom and Jeffrey were resorting to buying me like I was Alison. I didn't think so. A new hairdo, huh? I was about to get a hairdo they'd never forget.

The minute I got to *Blink,* I made an appointment

for lunchtime at a supertrendy hair salon in SoHo. I begged Jen to come with me; she was thrilled. At the appointed hour Henri (no last name, thank you) stood behind me, giving my head a surgeon's once-over. He pulled at several strands of my lank, tree-trunk brown hair and shook his head.

Disgruntled but hopeful, I let Henri color and snip at my hair. I wanted him to transform me into someone dangerous. Someone who would make Jeffrey and Alison gasp in horror. Someone who would remind Daniel that I could be as wild and interesting as any folksinger named Suki. Jen sat in the waiting area, letting the receptionists bring her herbal tea and copies of *Vogue* magazine. Finally Henri pronounced me, his creation, officially done.

"Voilà!" he said, whipping the chair around to give me the full view. I didn't recognize the girl staring back. She wore a jet black, layered bob that ended at her chin. It was way severe. In fact, I looked like the love child of Christina Ricci and Elvira, Mistress of the Dark. I couldn't tell whether I loved it or hated it. Jen and Henri were both gaga over it.

"Omigod. You are so chic. It's like when Gwyneth went brunette." Leave it to Jen to make the celeb connection.

"You really like it?" I asked, biting my lip. My skin looked a little washed out under all that black hair. Then again, I *had* asked for something radical.

"I love it," Jen said, wrapping her arm through mine. "Now, let's go shopping. New hair demands new clothes and new makeup."

Jen took me to her favorite ultrahip clothing store in SoHo. I left wearing a vinyl, leopard-print raincoat that was sort of a mix between campy and classy and gold hoop earrings. They looked pretty goofy with my J. Crew khakis and white K-Swiss tennis shoes. But it was a start.

"Come on," Jen said. "Let's get back to *Blink* and show them the new Lindsay DeWitt."

Ann was the first one to lay eyes on the new me. I could tell she liked the old me better, even if she didn't say so. "Wow. Look at you. It's quite a change."

We were standing in the hall, drawing a crowd. Even the mail guys did a double take. I wasn't so sure I liked being the center of attention. It was Alison's style, not mine. But judging from the reactions I was getting, I was sure to tick off Jeffrey and Mom and start them on the path to disagreeing on what to do next. Hopefully it would be enough time for Mom to come to her senses, and the whole wedding nightmare could be called off.

I walked tall around the corner and down the long hall to my office, trying not to pay attention to the stares I was getting from my coworkers. I saw Daniel coming down the hall, and my breath caught in my chest. Would he think I was some hot new intern, a woman of mystery? Would he even notice? He looked my way and cocked his head to one side, trying to register the sight. He drew closer, and his eyes were the size of half-dollars.

"Whoa. DeWitt, is that you?"

Was that a good "whoa" or a bad "whoa"? I didn't notice any outward signs of palpitations or other sudden love feelings, not that I would know what to look for. "Yep, it's me," I said. "You think it's enough to make Mom and Jeffrey go ballistic?"

"I think it's enough to have them send you to military school overnight."

The urge to fish for a compliment was getting unbearable. I baited that hook and sent it flying. "What do you think?"

"I think after last time, I'm not making comments on makeovers." My hook splashed in the water without a single nibble. Talk about bummers. Maybe I needed red lipstick. It always worked for Winona Ryder.

"Hey, listen, I had a great time last night, wacky paparazzi and all. Thanks." Daniel had his hands in his pockets. He rocked back and forth on his heels like a first grader. I was smitten to the tenth power.

"Yeah, me too. I gotta give you your jacket. Don't let me forget." I hoped he wouldn't be able to tell I had slept in it.

"Sure. I can just get it from you tomorrow. Hey, what time are we leaving?"

The whole crew was heading out to the Hamptons tomorrow. "I'm not sure. I think sometime in the evening. Mom hates traffic."

"Cool. So I'll call you tomorrow to set the Bat time. Oh, hey, so I want to show you what I'm following up on Forrester. It's all I've found."

I followed Daniel to an empty conference room, where he showed me an article about Jeffrey's ties to a judge in Mississippi who'd been sent to prison five years ago. There was a photo of Jeffrey shaking hands with the judge just a few months before the man was convicted of embezzlement. Aha! Once my mom found out about Jeffrey's tie to a criminal, it would be bye-bye, Jeffrey and Alison Forrester and their cell phones and lap dogs and twenty-four-carat gold toilet-paper holders. And Mom and I could go back to the way things were.

I gave Daniel an impulsive kiss on the forehead. He looked stunned.

"What was that for?"

"For saving my life. I totally owe you." What I wanted to do was kiss him smack on his shy smile of a mouth.

"That's okay. You're giving me a ride to the Hamptons, remember?"

Right. A ride to the Hamptons.

And The Dock.

And Suki.

I hadn't even put the two together! How could I have been so stupid? Of course that was why Daniel was going with me to the wedding. Because he needed a ride to some club in East Hampton. To see Suki sing.

For a minute it hurt to breathe.

"I remember," was all I said.

I sulked all the way home. I sat on the couch in our living room with a bowl of vanilla Swiss almond mixed with Cherry Garcia. Only forty-eight hours till the double whammy of inevitable: Mom's wedding and Suki. I was hoping I could stop one, but could I do anything to stop the other?

Consuela came through with a load of towels, took one look at my new hair, and made the sign of the cross. I was going to need all the protection I could get once Mom saw me.

At seven-fifteen she and Jeffrey waltzed in, arm in arm and laughing about something that had just happened in the street. I waited for them to notice. It didn't take long.

Mom stood staring at me for what seemed an eternity, then she burst into tears. "What have you done to your hair? Your beautiful, beautiful hair?"

I had expected fireworks and big, noisy finger-pointing, not tears. The crying only made me feel guilty. I'm one of those people guilt was made for—it always works on me.

"H-He told me to g-get my hair done!" I stammered, pointing to Jeffrey. Good to know I was handling it in a mature fashion.

Jeffrey put his arm around Mom, who was now sobbing. Alison breezed through the door and stopped mid-cell phone call. That was a first. "What. Did. You. Do. To your hair?"

"Colored it. What did you do to yours?"

Alison flashed me an evil look. "I am not going to Mortimer's with that freak show on the couch over there, Daddy."

"Alison, stop it." Jeffrey's voice was firm with-

122

out being mean. He tried to comfort my mom. "Now, honey, I did tell Lindsay to do whatever she wanted. Maybe I should have been more specific." He smiled, and Mom sort of laughed, then cried harder. "Well, I think she looks terrific." He said it like the captain of a sinking ship ordering the band to keep playing.

Mom looked at him through tearstained eyes. Alison gasped and stormed out of the room. You could have knocked me over with a flea. Jeffrey was coming to my defense? "I like it that she's not afraid to try different things and to march to her own drummer. That's the kind of girl who becomes a success. Mark my words."

Jeffrey was saving me, and I was ready to take him under. My guilt reached new lows. Mom, however, was not as forgiving.

"I want you to go upstairs right now and put on something nice for dinner, Lindsay Jane." Wow. She'd used both names. She was really steamed. "And I don't want you to see that Daniel Newman boy ever again."

It was like I'd been kicked in the chest. She couldn't ban me from Daniel. He was the best thing that had happened to me the whole lousy month.

It was the truth. He was.

"Mom!" I said, drawing it out into five syllables. "You can't do that. He's my date to the wedding."

"Not anymore, he's not. Not after the way you've been acting since you started seeing him. I think he's a bad influence."

"It's not Daniel. It's me, okay? Look, you can ground me till I'm in dentures, but please don't do this. I mean, the wedding is this weekend. What am I going to do for a date?"

"We'll find someone to take his place. But you are not to see him, and that's final. Jeffrey, I think we should go ahead and leave first thing in the morning. I don't want to wait and see what other surprises are in store. Now, I want you to call that boy right now and tell him you're sorry, but you will be finding another date."

"That's not fair to him!" I said. "He'll have to rearrange his whole—"

"Pick up that phone this instant, young lady!"

Mom stood and watched while I dialed his telephone number. Mr. Newman answered. "Mr. Newman? This is Lindsay DeWitt. Is Daniel home? He's not?" I flashed Mom a hopeful look. She mouthed to me to leave a message. "Could I leave a message? Could you tell him that I'm sorry, but I'm going to have to find another date to the wedding this weekend? Yes, please tell him I'll explain it all later. Thank you."

Oh God. Oh God. Oh God. What would Daniel think?

"Excuse me," I bit out. "I've got to put on something suitable to wear to our suitable dinner so you suitable people won't be embarrassed to be seen with me."

I knew I'd hurt my mom, but I couldn't believe

she was doing this to me. I didn't even have time to see Daniel and try to make it all better now that we were leaving for Jeffrey's estate in the Hamptons tomorrow morning. I had to get word to him.

Twenty minutes later I snuck downstairs with a small bundle and handed it to Consuela.

"Consuela, there's a messenger service coming to pick this up. Can you give it to them? And please don't tell Mom." Consuela cluck-clucked her tongue, but I knew she couldn't resist indulging me, whether it was an extra cookie after dinner or helping me deliver vital info to a guy I was bonkers about.

And I really was bonkers about Daniel. There was no way around it.

I only hoped it wasn't too late.

Eleven

Daniel

WHEN I SAW the front page of the *New York Post*—the one that featured a table-dancing Lindsay and a doofy-looking me—taped to my closed bedroom door, I knew it was going to be a rough night. I opened the door to my sanctuary only to find Dad sitting on the edge of my unmade bed. I couldn't tell what he wanted to do first, lecture me or fold my laundry.

"That's quite an impression you made on the *Post*'s photographers." His jaw was clenching and unclenching. Not a good sign.

"You know, Daniel, your mother and I did not raise you to become some airhead party boy."

I picked some socks off the floor and shoved them in a drawer. "Leave Mom out of this, okay?"

"I don't want you hanging around Lindsay DeWitt. She's trouble. Her whole family is trouble.

Her mother's been married five times—"

"Four," I corrected.

"And she's marrying that weasel Jeffrey Forrester this weekend in a wedding that is costing enough money to feed a Third World country. It's obscene."

I tried to fold a shirt, but it kept falling apart. I rolled it up and shoved it in another drawer. "Lindsay's not like most rich people. She's different. You met her."

"Yes. But she wasn't dancing on the tables at the time."

"Dad, you had to be there. It was totally my fault. I provoked her into doing it."

"I appreciate your trying to be honorable about it, but that's the way these people operate, son. They draw you in over your head, and then they let you take the rap on the front of the *New York Post*."

"Not Lindsay," I said, throwing my sneakers in my overfilled closet. A tennis racket and some snow boots started to fall down from the top shelf, but I managed to close the door fast. I felt them stop, midthump, against the closet door.

"You're sure about that?"

"Yeah, I'm sure." I really wanted to win against Dad, just once. "In fact, we're working on an exposé of Jeffrey Forrester right now. I found out some pretty interesting dirt, and Lindsay's gonna spring it on him. There probably won't even be a wedding."

Dad's eyes got all crinkly, and he smiled. It

wasn't an I'm-proud-of-you smile. It was a sad smile. "Or maybe she's warning Jeffrey."

I was totally confused. "What do you mean?"

"Lindsay called here earlier. She said to tell you that she was sorry, but she was taking another date to the wedding."

The walls seemed to get narrower, and there was a hissing noise in my ears. I couldn't clear my head. "You're lying," I said, even though I knew my dad never lied about anything, even when you wanted him to.

"I'm sorry, Daniel. I really am."

So Lindsay had ditched me after all, and Dad thought I was a patsy. I could hear my mom's voice saying there's a sucker born every minute. More than anything, I wished she were here to make sense of everything, to make it better.

My throat ached with wanting to cry. And then I felt Dad standing behind me, wrapping his long arms around me. My whole body tensed, then let go. With Dad anchoring me in place, I cried hard—over Mom, over Lindsay, over the two years of not letting Dad in, over every hope I hadn't been able to save. When it was over, I was totally spent.

"Thanks," I mumbled.

Dad's voice was catching too. "I love you, Dan-Dan."

He hadn't called me that since I was riding a trike, and I almost lost it again, but I didn't want to drown in snot, so I pulled it together. "Do you mind if I just kind of hang out here? I think I need to be alone."

Dad ruffled my head and closed the door softly behind him. Once I got past the weepies, I realized I was thoroughly angry at Lindsay. Not only had she dissed me, but now I was short a ride to see Suki. Suki. There was a stand-up kind of girl. My renewed mission in life was to make her fall in love with me and to rub it in Lindsay's rich-girl face. I was sure Suki even loved hockey.

Somehow, some way, I was going to East Hampton.

Dad knocked on my door and poked in his head. "This just came for you." He lobbed a package at me. "By messenger too. Very mysterious."

Huh. It was a big brown package with no return address. I grabbed some scissors and ripped it open. My jacket was in there, tied around some other stuff: detailed directions to East Hampton, enough cash for a train ticket, cab fare once I got there, instructions, and a note.

> Dear Daniel,
>   I am sooo sorry about all of this. No time to explain. Don't try to call, as Mom and Jeffrey think you're a "bad influence" (direct quote). I promise it will all work out. Just use the enclosed to get to East Hampton as fast as you can. We have got to stop this wedding. Okay?
>   Love,
>   Lindsay

Somebody actually thought I, mild-mannered Daniel Newman, was a bad influence. Cool! This was so major. And was it my imagination, or had Lindsay signed the note *love?* And what did that mean, exactly? And why did I care? I'd have time to ponder it on the train ride out there. The fact was, I was about to get everything I ever wanted—a chance to work on my big story, time to help Lindsay, and a hot date with the girl of my dreams, Suki. There was nothing complicated about Suki. I'd show up, she'd sing, and then we'd go to the beach and get to know each other, like she said. It'd be great. There'd be no fights, no "bad influencing," no . . . no problems, like there were with Lindsay.

I raced down the hall and pushed Dad off the couch and toward the front door. "What are you doing?" he asked, grabbing for his keys.

"I'll explain on the way. I need you to do something for me. It's important, okay?"

"Do you mind at least telling me where we're going?"

"To the Lower East Side. Al's Discount Tux Shop. Come on. We've got one hour before they close."

Lindsay

It was like black curtains hanging from either side of my head.

That's what the horrible hair-don't looked like the next morning. I had made the biggest mistake of my life letting Henri do his radical act on my style-challenged hair. I hated it beyond words. But I couldn't give in and fix it now after all the trouble it had caused me. If Mom wouldn't let Daniel be my date, then I was letting the evil hair stand. It was my badge of dishonor.

I put my Cover Girl compact mirror away in my backpack and took a good look at Jeffrey's modest little cottage in East Hampton: a four-acre, ten-million-dollar spread that made the Taj Mahal look quaint. And in the center of it all stood his crowning glory, Belle Reve. The thing was ultramodern.

"Don't you just love this place?" Mom trilled.

I couldn't figure out where the doorknobs were. There were these long, cylindrical, dangling tubes. First you had to catch one. Then you had to figure out how to open the door.

Jeffrey stepped ahead of me and just pushed open the door. Oh. Immediately a handful of servants came running to take our things. It made me feel really weird. Inside, the place seemed like an airplane hangar. The ceilings reached up to the sky. Everything was extremely modern. He had white, space-age chairs and mobiles from the Museum of Modern Art. I was having a hard time imagining us in our sweet pink silk dresses and Mom in her ivory walking around in this fun house. But once I looked outside, I saw how truly beautiful it was. They had set up billowing, white tents all across the lawn. Beyond perfect hedges and a duck pond, I could see the ocean, calm and gray-blue. It was exactly the place for a fairy-tale wedding. And I was starting to feel like the evil stepsister.

I couldn't tell if my deep blues were the result of (*a*) my mom marrying Jeffrey, who was probably a no-good schemer, (*b*) having to spend way too much time with Alison and her ever present cell phone, or (*c*) missing Daniel. The answer was probably (*d*), all of the above, but I couldn't get Daniel off my mind. I hoped that he had gotten my package and that he didn't hate me for all time. I thought about e-mailing him, but if he was coming, he had to be on his way right now, and he wouldn't get it. My mind was swirling with so many thoughts and feelings. I wanted to be with Daniel, but only if he didn't want to be with Suki. I wanted him to want me. Maybe I should just ask him about her. No.

I saw Mom heading down one side of the double-spiral staircase. I ran down and around the other, trying to catch up with her. I had to tell her about Jeffrey now before things went any further.

"Mom," I yelled. "Wait up!"

"Hi, sweetie," Mom said, still walking at her breakneck pace.

"Can I talk to you for a sec?"

"Sure, honey. I just have to meet with Connor about some of the details." Connor was Mom's wedding coordinator. He was from Beverly Hills, and he thought everything was fabulous. He was in serious danger of having a fabulous OD.

"This is sort of important," I said. We stepped into a massive library with shelves that looked straight out of a futuristic warehouse. They were actually suspended from the ceiling on silvery wires. I bumped one and felt it wobble a bit.

Mom plopped down in an orange chair in the shape of a kidney. I sat on a big stuffed llama chair nearby. "I need to tell you something about Jeffrey. Something I think you need to know before you go through with this wedding . . ."

"Something about Jeffrey?" Mom repeated in a totally distracted way.

"Yes, it seems that Jeffrey—"

"Ah, there you are. *Fab-u-lous!*" Connor rushed into the room in his pin-striped suit, carrying his master book filled with flowers, swatches, rings, you name it.

He kissed both of Mom's cheeks and looked at me strangely. "I like your hair. It's very SoHo. *Fabulous.* Caroline, we simply *must* talk to the gardeners about shearing that hedge a bit over by the duck pond. It's looking a little shaggy."

"I'll tell Jeffrey," Mom said. "How is the cake coming along?"

If he said "fabulous," I was going to scream. "Well, you know I have to stand over those boys in the kitchen with a whip, but I think you are going to love it, love it, love it. And we've gotten the most *gorgeous* fresh wildflowers to press into it. It's a dream."

Mom's face lit up like a little kid's. She was obviously having a great time, fussing over all the details. But I couldn't let her marry Jeffrey. Not until she had all the details and could make up her own mind.

"Mom, that thing I needed to tell you?" I looked meaningfully at her and gave Connor a sideways glance.

"Say no more. Connor is gone." He packed up his master book and stood off to the side, yelling at the florist on his cell phone.

I took a deep breath. "Okay, the thing is—"

Alison came tearing into the room in her bridesmaid dress, a worried seamstress following on her heels. "Caroline. Connor. You've got to do something about this dress!"

Connor came rushing over. "Darling, what is the matter? You look *fabulous*."

"Oh no. No, I do not think so. I think we left fabulous at the altar when someone"—she gave a backward glance at the seamstress—"raised the neckline a full inch. It makes me look flat chested. I need a bit of cleavage action, okay?"

The Russian seamstress was outraged. "Iss *nyet* proper for young lady to show bosom."

Connor put his arm around the lady. "Now, Olena, Miss Forrester's father, may I remind you, is paying for your services. And she would like the bodice lowered just a little bit. Be a good girl."

"Hmphf. Not proper." Olena marched out of the room, and Alison smiled her victory smile.

"Thanks, Connor. You're a doll. Oh, Lindsay. By the way, your date is here."

Daniel had made it already? I needed a chance to

hide him before Mom saw him and banished him to Verona or at least New Jersey. Alison motioned for me to follow her. Mom was already in deep discussion with Connor over the napkins, so I decided our talk would have to wait.

Alison led me to a side porch where Marlon was talking to some six-foot-two-inch blond god. He looked like he could be the cover of an Abercrombie & Fitch catalog. In fact, he was the cover of an Abercrombie & Fitch catalog. That's where I had seen him before.

"Oh, hi, Lindsay," Marlon said as I walked up. "This is me mate from my modeling agency, Sven. 'E's a bloke from Sweden. Doesn't speak much English, but 'e understands you're 'is date for this shindig."

"My date?" Okay, the guy was drop-dead gorgeous, but the no-English factor was a problem. Then again, considering my recent luck with guys, maybe it was a plus if he couldn't understand what I was saying.

"Nice meet to you." Sven extended a large, perfect hand. I shook it. No sparks. There was more going on in Daniel's quirky pinkie than in this guy's whole beautiful bod.

Marlon led Sven off to his car to check out the DVD player in the backseat, and Alison and I were alone on the porch of the ugliest estate known to mankind. I so did not want to be her stepsister. In fact, I didn't want to be in the same county with her, let alone the same family.

136

Alison leaned back in a deck chair made of teak and some kind of metal bolts. I couldn't tell whether it was really a chair or a sculpture. "Shame about Daniel," she said. "But really, it's better this way. Sven's better looking. He'll look great in the pictures, don't you think?"

As far as I was concerned, Sven the Swede couldn't even compare to Daniel in all his scruffy, adorable boyfulness. "I hear toothpaste will clear up a zit overnight. You might want to jump on that right away," I said, leaving the porch and striding across the massive lawn toward the water, where I could have some peace. It was a pretty meow thing to say, but hey, my days of fighting fair were over the minute Alison Forrester arrived on the scene. I could only hope and pray that Daniel would make it and I could put an end to this whole wedding nightmare before it was too late.

Twelve

Daniel

SOMETIMES YOU CAN be too rich.

That's what I was thinking when the cab pulled up to Belle Reve, the Forresters' estate in the Hamptons. Only a rich person could get away with having such a butt-ugly house and calling it an architectural marvel. No wonder Lindsay didn't want to do the old family-merge thing. Yikes.

I had the cab drop me off about a quarter mile from the place. There were so many news cameras and tabloid reporters hanging around that you could barely get through. I wasn't exactly sure how I was going to get past the beefy security guys. They were dressed in black suits with little electronic things in their ears. When they've got the accessories, you know they're serious. Lindsay hadn't mentioned security in her instructions. I was gonna be pretty p.o.'ed if I'd come all this way for nothing.

I still needed a ride to The Dock, which, as best as I could tell, was a good fifteen miles away—too far to walk.

A couple of the reporters seemed to be staring at me until I realized they were actually looking behind me. I heard a buzzing sound, like a motorcycle on helium, coming from down the road. A small blue scooter was toot-tooting its way toward us. The paparazzi started snapping away. The only thing I could make out was a big Ken doll of a guy with some girl hanging on for dear life behind him. They zoomed closer, and I could make out Lindsay crouching on the seat behind the blond-hair-big-teeth dude.

"That's her," one of the reporters shouted.

"Oh, man. I have to reload," another yelled back.

I still couldn't get over the fact that Lindsay had her arms around what had to be a set of washboard abs. The guy was huge. And he had very large, very white teeth. Also, he looked like he could kick my butt without breaking a sweat. I hated him on sight. The blue Vespa scooter slowed down as it reached me, and Lindsay shouted to me over the motor.

"Cousin Daniel! So glad you could make it all the way from California! I'm sorry Jeeves forgot to pick you up at the airport." The girl was quick. I had to give her that. "Here," she said, climbing off the scooter. "You ride in with Sven, and I'll follow you."

Was she out of her twisted mind? Me, ride

behind the bohunk? "Uh, I think I'll just walk."

"Oh no, Cousin Daniel. I insist," Lindsay said, giving me a warning look and a boost onto the bike. She took my tux bag out of my hands. Sven peeled out, and I instinctively grabbed at his waist with both arms to steady myself. I really hoped that shot wouldn't make the papers, or I'd have to change schools.

Lindsay finally broke through the reporters with the help of Fric and Frac of security. She raced up the lawn with my tux bag flying out behind her like a kite. "Cousin Daniel," she said, giving me a wink and a hug that made me feel a little warm. "Sven, this is my cousin."

Sven looked uncomprehendingly at us. He smiled and nodded fiercely. "Can you wait for us in the house? I have to show my cousin . . . er, my favorite horse. In the stables. Right, Dan? Didn't you say how much you wanted to meet . . . Flicka?"

"Sure," I played along. "Dying to meet that Flicka. That old sweet mare."

Sven pointed to the house and muttered something in Swedish, waved good-bye, and headed toward the duck pond. I took my tux bag from Lindsay. "Okay. I see 'wait in the house' translated in Sven-speak to 'go over to the duck pond.'"

"Whatever," Lindsay said, showing me the way to the stables. "I am sooo glad to see you."

So she was glad to see me? Relieved glad or special glad? I was pretty glad to see her too.

The sun was just setting over the water, and the

141

sky was muting into a pinky-blue with indigo edges. Soon the stars would be winking at us overhead, letting us in on the joke that they'd been dead for millions of years but still put on a great light show. I wondered which star was Mom's. Was she out there, watching me missing her?

"You okay?" Lindsay put her hand on my shoulder like I might be sick or something.

"Yeah. Fine. I was just thinking. My mom really loved weddings. She'd think this was a gas."

We were quiet for a minute. Just stood there, waiting for night to come on shift. One, two, three lights blinked on in the house. A maid came out to light citronella candles in bags along the front walkway. Before we knew it, dusk had cleared the way for the moon to come on in full glory. I liked it that Lindsay didn't say anything. She just let the moment be. When the full moon rose and sat in the sky, she led the way to the stables again.

"They'll be looking for me soon. Tonight's the rehearsal dinner." I could tell she was feeling pretty lousy about the whole wedding. I guess both of us were out of sorts.

The stables were deserted, thankfully, except for the horses. A chestnut horse with a white spot on her nose took a liking to me and started nibbling at my Red Hot Chili Peppers T-shirt. I moved away. As a city boy, I wasn't feeling the I'm-at-one-with-nature vibe. "Do you mind? This is my favorite concert T-shirt."

Lindsay patted the horse on the nose. "I'm sorry

everything's been so messed up. I know it was a big hassle getting here and all. I hope you don't hate me."

"I don't hate you. But the weekend's still young." I could tell she felt bad about everything.

"I'm working on Mom and the Sven thing. I think I can break her down and convince her to let you be my date after all. She's so whacked-out with last minute wedding plans that she'd probably let me bring a criminal as my date. Not that I'm implying anything."

"Glad to hear it. I thought you were gonna make me hold up a bank next or something." I laughed. "So when are you telling your mom about Jeffrey?"

She sat on the stable floor and hugged her knees to her chest. Across the lawn I could hear someone calling her name. "I haven't had a chance, but I will. Even if I have to do it when the minister asks if anyone present objects to the marriage."

"Whoa. That's pretty harsh, Lindsay." The voices calling Lindsay's name were getting closer.

She picked up a piece of straw and made swirls in the dirt floor with it. "I thought you were on my side."

"I am. It's just that, you know, if it goes that far, then I think you gotta let it go. It's too cold to just announce it during the wedding all Aaron Spelling style."

Lindsay jumped up and put her hands on her hips. She was working up to full lather. "So now you're saying I'm turning into a drama queen?

Excuse me, but who found the dirt on Jeffrey in the first place?"

Now I understood what they meant about killing the messenger. "Oh, man, you cannot blame that on me. I was helping you out."

"Well, don't do me any favors, Newman."

"Look, all I'm saying is that we should do some fact checking—"

Lindsay cut me off. "And another thing—"

"Maybe," I yelled over her, "you should talk to Jeffrey first. Ask him what the deal is."

". . . you always do this to me . . . change your mind and—"

"Lindsay—"

". . . then I feel totally confused, and it's hard enough—"

"Lindsay—"

". . . to figure out the right thing to do without—"

I pulled Lindsay into me with everything I had, and the next thing I knew, my mouth was on hers and we were falling into a kiss like you read about in stories you never believe. It wasn't just a smooch. This was a full-on, neither-one-wants-to-end-it kiss. Lindsay finally wrapped her arms across my back. I had one hand around her waist, and the other was at the back of her head. The feel of her silky hair in my fingers was making my whole arm tingle.

I couldn't stop kissing her. There was a humming going on inside my head that turned into a pop and a bang like firecrackers going off. The sky went white, and little sparkly tears of light rained down through the trees followed by a red, white, and blue explosion. There *were* firecrackers going off. Real ones. I could hear guests oohing and aahing over the display. But they couldn't touch the firecracker of a kiss Lindsay and I had just shared. Lindsay pulled away, and I wanted her back so bad, it hurt.

Someone called her name—someone who was only a few yards from the stables. It sounded like Alison. "I better run before they find us," she said, all out of breath. She looked strangely flushed and beautiful with the flashing firecracker light playing across her face like a movie.

"Yeah, sure," I said, stepping back and putting my hands in my pockets to keep from reaching for her again.

"I'll be back later," she said. She kissed me quickly on the mouth and ran off toward the oohs and aahs and bottled stars exploding over our heads.

I leaned back against a stall and let the chestnut horse nibble away at my collar. It was frayed anyway. It was very simple: I was supposed to come to the Hamptons, help Lindsay undo a wedding, then ride off into the sunset with Suki, the girl of my dreams.

How had I managed to screw it up so royally? *Suki* was my dream girl. Not Lindsay. But if that was the case, then why did Lindsay's kiss make me want to do cartwheels across Belle Reve's massive lawn? I was going to end up hurting Lindsay and feeling horrible about it. But maybe, just for tonight, it was all right to feel Lindsay in the air around me.

I left the love-struck mare while I still had a T-shirt left and snuck off to watch the rehearsal party down by the water. At first I didn't see her. Then she came down the sloping lawn, wearing a long, yellow sundress. If you looked past the bad dye job and haircut, she looked like a princess.

Far above her head firecrackers exploded and screeched. And a little above that, a superbright star twinkled at me. If I didn't know better, I'd swear it was Mom, checking out the wedding of the year and her son's first taste of a kiss that meant something. Like I said, if I didn't know better.

Lindsay

Did you ever have one of those kisses that you could swear has just totally rewired parts of your brain? Like speech, for instance? By the time I came stumbling out of the stables on new foal legs with my lips freshly kissed, I could barely find words to talk to Marlon, Alison, and Sven, who had all come looking for me. The kiss was so spectacular, I was even able to overlook the fact that Alison was in a royal snit because I was late to the rehearsal dinner.

"You know, there are such things as watches and manners," she said, taking a break from a phone call with one of the other teen witches in her fashion coven.

"Sorry. Guess I lost track of time," I said with this completely goofy grin on my face.

"What's your damage? Why are you smiling like that? Oh my God. Have you been doing drugs? No, Tiff, I wasn't talking to you." Alison sighed into her phone.

I refused to let Miss Snip ruin my amazing, float-ten-feet-above-the-ground mood. "Can't a girl just be in a good mood?"

"Bloody right, Lindsay bird," Marlon said, placing an arm around my shoulders like a brother. He might be dumb as a post, but he had a good heart. "It sure beats the old mope from this morning, eh?"

Okay. Maybe he didn't have to be quite so forthcoming. Marlon leaned in and whispered in my ear, "Whaddya think of me mate Sven, then? The girls are mad for 'im. Can see why, can' I? I think he really fancies you, luv."

The last thing in the world I wanted was to have Sven mooning over me.

"He's a nice guy, but I wouldn't start planning to dance at our wedding just yet."

I excused myself to get dressed, but mostly I just wanted time alone to go over that kiss with Daniel in deliciously agonizing mental slo-mo. The fact was, *he* had kissed *me*. I hadn't done anything. One minute we were arguing, and the next his mouth was on mine, turning my insides all hot and achy.

And now my brain wouldn't work right. All systems were computing to Daniel and nothing but Daniel. I put on my sundress; I was putting it on for Daniel. I brushed my hair; I felt Daniel's fingers on my neck. I spritzed perfume; I smelled Daniel on my skin. And tomorrow it would all be over and he would run off to be with Suki. And worse, I would drive him to meet her. Why had I ever made such a stupid deal in the first place?

All through the rehearsal dinner I was itchy and distracted. I barely touched my filet mignon, and steak does it for me in a big way. I'm a real carnivore. But tonight my stomach was too jittery to handle food. I was nervous about telling Mom her dream boat was sinking, and I was desperate to think of a way to stop Daniel from going to Suki.

When the dessert plates were brought around, the band began to play "Moon River." That's one of Mom's favorite romantic songs. It doesn't do anything for me, but then, I'm not over the age of forty either. Jeffrey kissed Mom's hand and headed straight for me. I was hoping against hope that he wouldn't ask me to dance, but no luck.

"Lindsay, would you indulge an old man who'd like to dance with a beautiful young girl?" He held out his hand to me like an old-fashioned gentleman. A lump was forming in the back of my throat. In fact, it was hard to talk at all.

"Me?" I croaked.

"Who else?" He smiled and led me to the dance floor. I don't know a whole lot about slow dancing.

Jeffrey was pretty good at it, though. I could tell he'd had to dance a lot in his life, probably at lots of parties and stuff. We swept around the dance floor. Jeffrey kept his hand on my back the way professional dance instructors do when they're trying to get you to follow. I was surprised at how easy it was to dance while he was helping me.

"So tell me . . . how do you really feel about being my stepdaughter, Lindsay? Now, don't worry. Whatever you say will be strictly confidential. I won't tell your mother a thing." He looked me right in the eye and smiled. For a guy who was supposed to be crooked, he had an amazingly straight smile.

If my heart could have beat any faster, it would have drowned out the band. It was now or never. "I . . . the thing is . . ." I cleared my throat and went for it. "I know some stuff about you. About your 'association' with Judge Bastrop—a convicted criminal."

Jeffrey's smile disappeared. I was really scared. Would he yell at me? Leave me on the dance floor? Instead he just kept dancing, but his eyes were far away. "I knew you were an ace journalist."

Ouch. A compliment. I was starting to feel unsure of myself. But I'd come so far, and I'd made Daniel do all that work. I couldn't back down now.

"Lindsay, this may sound hard to believe, but you've got the wrong idea about it. It's a long story, an important one, and I could explain it to you later, when your mom and I get back from our honeymoon."

"If there *is* a honeymoon, you mean. I know my mom is kind of impulsive, and maybe she doesn't have the best track record with husbands, but she's still my mom." Two tears plopped over onto my cheeks, and I wiped them away with the back of my hand. "I won't let her get hurt!"

The music stopped, and Jeffrey escorted me over to an empty table. He brought me a cup of punch. I didn't want to drink it, but I was thirstier than I had known. We sat at the table while the band played a Motown song and the dance floor filled with people doing their thing. "I would never do anything to hurt your mother or you, Lindsay. I know you don't really know me yet. I know it's been hard on you having a dad who's never around. But I promise you, if you'll let me in, I'll take good care of both of you. I'm a little rough around the edges, but I'm not a bad guy."

I felt like I was drowning. I didn't know which way to swim toward the surface. It was all just bubbles and panic and confusion. "I have to tell Mom. She needs to know everything."

Jeffrey played with the platinum cuff links on his shirt cuffs. They were monogrammed and simple. Obviously a gift from Mom. "You have to do what your conscience tells you to do, Linds. I wouldn't have it any other way."

The guy knew how to make you feel like a heel. That was for sure. He reached into his jacket pocket and pulled out a long, elegant silver box tied up in gold ribbon and placed it on the table in front of me. "What's this?" I asked warily.

"Just a little wedding present from me to you. I'd been waiting for the right moment to give it to you, but I guess now's as good a time as any. I should probably get back to the party." He gave me a kiss on the cheek just like a dad, and I thought I was going to burst out crying. I'd waited my whole life for my own dad to pay attention to me like that. Now I was getting that dad attention from a guy I was about to rat on. I was beyond miserable. I was heading into full-on indigo blues.

Jeffrey clapped some business guy on the back and acted like nothing was wrong. It's funny how adults can do that. The world can cave in, and they'll act like they're fine and dandy and ready to go to the beach with you. The silver package was taunting me there on the table. Part of me wanted to give it back, unopened. Maybe that was the honorable thing to do. But part of me was curious. And let's face it, curious always wins out over honorable. Otherwise we'd never have to read so many annoying stories where the moral comes right after the curious little children have been eaten by big, bad wolves and witches.

I peeled back the top and pulled off the cotton-packing fluff. There in the box was the most beautiful pen I had ever seen in my life. It was deep forest green with gold filigree around the tip. My initials were carved in the end. An ink cartridge was in the box too. It was an old-fashioned writing pen, the kind you see in antique stores. Just holding it between my fingers made me feel like a real writer.

There was a small note folded over and stuck in the side of the pen. It read: *Dear Lindsay, you are a great talent. Always believe in your dreams. Love, Jeffrey.*

Why couldn't he do something terrible like threaten to throw me in a convent in remote Canada so I could feel totally right about what I was doing? I looked around at the party guests, mostly Jeffrey's friends. I saw bored women in a lot of jewelry, talking about redecorating their summer homes, and men with cigars, gabbing about golf games and stock prices and mergers and acquisitions. No one was looking at the incredible night sky or thinking about a boy they had kissed who had left them feeling floaty and beautiful. These were the kinds of people Mom and I would have to see more often. It made me feel hollow inside. And then there was that perfect pen and note from Jeffrey.

I couldn't get my head around both thoughts at the same time. How was it possible for him to live in two separate worlds? How was it possible for him to be associated with a convicted politician and spend time with these selfish people and still be so sweet to my mom and me?

My head ached at the thought. Or maybe it was the fact that I hadn't eaten more than a handful of salted peanuts all night. I made my way to the buffet table and hoped that the answer lay in a stomach full of pasta salad and cold filet mignon.

Thirteen

Daniel

I WENT CAMPING once and thought it was the most uncomfortable twenty-four hours of my life. That was before I'd tried to sleep in a stable. The ground was cold, hard, and covered in dirt and straw. The horses have a way of snoring that makes you jump every five minutes. And let's not forget the lovely smell. All in all, not how I'd envisioned spending my weekend.

"Knock, knock." I jumped back to my hiding place behind an old watering trough, but then I saw it was Lindsay, holding what looked like a couple of blankets and some Tupperware that smelled a lot better than what I had been smelling.

"Hey," I said.

"Hey," she said back shyly. Here it came—the awkward first meeting after the big-bang kiss. Instead of wanting to run away, I had the urge to just sit and talk to her till morning. Maybe it was the fresh sea air or that bright star that made me think of Mom, but I was alive all over. Spending time with Lindsay made me use every part of myself. I couldn't just coast. A guy could get used to such a feeling.

I glanced at my watch. One-thirty in the morning. Lindsay offered me the Tupperware, and my stomach growled like an entire zoo. "What is it?"

"Eye of newt. Toad's tail. Bat's wings. The usual." She shrugged. She put the blankets down on the ground and made a little pallet for me. I plopped down and dug into the leftover party food with a plastic fork. Lindsay perched herself next to me, drawing her knees to her chest and wrapping her arms around her knees. She seemed a million miles away. I had been so starved that I dug in without saying a word. I swallowed a big mouthful of fruit salad.

"Everything okay in Lindsay land?"

"I can't do it."

"Yeah, most people have that reaction to watching me eat. It's not pretty. I'll understand if you need to avert your eyes."

She didn't laugh. "I mean I can't go through with exposing Jeffrey. I've been walking around since the rehearsal dinner ended, just thinking and watching the tide go back and forth."

I knew I should probably say something deep here, but going without food so long had left me a little light-headed. "Well, you sure know how to have a good time. Still, it can't be as boring as going to the ballet."

Lindsay put her head on my shoulder and started to cry softly. Nothing freaks a guy out more than having a girl cry on his shoulder. Especially when he's holding a plate of really tempting food. I did the noble thing and put down the food. Then I put my arms around Lindsay and tried not to be a total dork. I didn't want to say anything stupid or insensitive, so I opted for the strong, silent treatment. Lindsay's sobs settled down into little hiccups. She pulled away from my shoulder. I'd liked the feel of her there and wished she'd come back.

"I'm really sorry," she said, wiping at her eyes.

"For what?"

"For dragging you all the way out here for nothing. For ruining your big story about the judge after you worked so hard on it. I mean, I know you're supposed to be working on the profile on me and Alison."

The profile I still hadn't started and still didn't want to. Every time I thought I knew Lindsay, I found out I didn't.

I stared at the food getting cold and wondered if it would be unforgivable for me to eat the rest of it. "Don't worry about it. I was happy to help." I meant it. I'd been happier the past few weeks than I'd been in a long time. It had been exciting and fun.

Lindsay gave me a weak smile. There were runny mascara marks under her eyes, but I thought she was totally cute. "I'll repay you for the tux. And tomorrow morning I'll give you a ride out to The Dock so you can see Suki."

My heart gave this little convulsion, like a preview of a heart attack. "How did you know about Suki?"

"I saw that flyer in your notebook. She seems really cool."

"Yeah," I said. I didn't know what else to say. "Well, you can wait until after the wedding to give me the ride. I'm still your date, right?"

"I don't know." Lindsay sighed. "I think I should probably do the right thing and go out with this guy, Sven, and not cause any more trouble. Besides, I know you didn't come here just to be my date to a stupid nine-hour wedding."

But I did. At least, that was a big part of it. In some twisted part of my brain I had actually been looking forward to putting on that tux and seeing Lindsay's reaction. I'd been thinking about how nice it would feel to slow dance just once with her with the ocean so close, you could touch it. "Yeah, right." I laughed. "You know me—I'm a real sucker for weddings." Something in me was turning cold and hard. Maybe Dad was right—if you got attached to rich people, they'd dump you first chance they got.

I stood up and made a big point of yawning. "I'm pretty beat, and you should go in. What time should I look for you?"

"Did I say something wrong?" Lindsay started

to put her hand on my chest. I moved back.

"No. I'm cold and tired. No biggie." No biggie. Hadn't she said that to me before?

"Sure." She wrapped her arms around herself like she needed a hug and that was the only way she knew how to get it. "I'll see you early. Around eight o'clock. Daniel?"

"Hmmm?" I gobbled down some more food. It turned to ash in my stomach.

"Nothing." Lindsay walked away slowly. I didn't go after her. I didn't stop her. I just kept my head down and told myself it was better this way.

Even if I didn't believe it for a minute.

Lindsay

At first I couldn't sleep. Then when I did, I had these bizarro dreams that I was running through a disco where everyone was Sven—the waitresses, the DJ, the dancers. I vowed never to eat that late ever again.

Had Daniel dreamed? Had he dreamed about me? He'd seemed so cold last night. Confusion was becoming my normal state of being. First there was that knockout kiss that made me want to do the happy-girl dance like I was the star in the opening credits of some sappy WB show. Then he just turned it off again. I knew he probably felt guilty because of the whole Suki thing.

Suki. Just saying her name made me want to throw darts at something—anything. It was seven o'clock on the nose. There was no putting this off. I brushed the little sweaters off my pearly whites and found Daniel in the stables. The blankets were folded up, and he was trying to stretch. He had to be pretty sore from sleeping on the ground. I refused to act like a wounded puppy.

"Hi!" I said, putting enough perky in my voice to be a telemarketer for a coffee chain. "Brought you a cinnamon roll. I'll say one thing about Jeffrey: He hired a mean cook."

Daniel took the cinnamon roll in its Ziploc bag. "I'll eat it later. Not much of an early morning food guy."

"Did you sleep okay?" What I really meant was, did you think about me?

"Yeah, sure. I think Bessie the chestnut mare is starting to get ideas about me, though. Maybe I should leave before she gets too attached."

I didn't know if her name was really Bessie, but I did know how she felt.

Daniel and I piled into Mom's Mercedes and snuck the car out the back way, where there weren't a horde of reporters staked out. We drove silently along a small, snaky road that gave an awesome view of the Atlantic Ocean on one side and the occasional mansion on the other. Once we hit the highway, we rolled open our windows and let the cool morning breeze whip through our hair. Before long the side of the road started getting thicker with bagel shops and antique stores, and I knew we were close to town. It felt so weird, so horrible, delivering Daniel to another girl.

The Dock was a little off the beaten path. As its name implied, it sat on a big pier. It was a pretty cute place that served basic grub and showcased music in the evenings. I wished I could just blow off this stupid wedding and spend the day here with Daniel. We could run along the beach and have a clambake and make sand castles and—

"Omigod, you made it!" A low, raspy voice broke into my little fantasy scene. Through the windshield I saw this totally sexy pixie girl running over to Daniel's side of the car. I recognized her from the flyer in Daniel's notebook and guessed she was the infamous Suki. When she threw her arms around Daniel and gave him a huge smooch on the mouth, I didn't need to guess at all. I had never been so jealous in my whole dateless life. Big green eyes, flawless skin, and tiny gymnast's body. I felt like a truck driver just being in the same airspace with her. She had on these ancient Levi's that were cut off just below the knees and this strappy little tank top. Definitely a cool chick.

Daniel was yapping away about taking the train out here and sleeping in the stable and all his adventures. He and Suki looked like, well, like a couple. And I know the saying about three being a crowd. Besides, I'm not very good with good-byes.

"I better get back before they send a search party," I yelled over crunching gravel. "Catch you later."

For a split second I thought Daniel made a move to get back in the car, but it must have been my eyes going all wonky in the bright sun. It was going to be a sunny, gorgeous day. And I had never felt lousier.

When I got back to the house, Mom was sitting in the living room, waiting for me. "Where have you been? I've been worried sick."

I cut her off before she could get all uppity and bring on the lecture and call me by my full name again. "I needed some time to think. Sorry. I should have left a note. Mom?"

"Yes?"

"Do you think it's too late to do something about my hair?"

Mom's face stopped looking so tired. She broke into a heart-melting grin and gave me one of her patented big kisses on the top of the head. She smelled like home. "Linds, honey, it's never too late for anything."

The Esther Salon took pity on us and worked me in right away. Esther herself evaluated my jet black mess of a do and gave me the bad news. "Darling, I can dye your hair back, but it will be very damaged. We'll have to cut it short."

I had never had short hair. I'd been wearing it the same way since kindergarten. It was the only security blanket I had left. But I didn't have much choice. "Okay," I said meekly. "Do what you have to do."

I couldn't bear to watch, so I kept my eyes closed while she snipped. Chunks of hair fell past my shoulders like rain. Some of it landed in my hands, and I ran my fingers over the rough strands of my past life.

Finally Esther pronounced me done. "Take a look," she said.

I saw my eyes first. All this time I'd thought they were sort of average, but now I could see they were really pretty. Big and brown and soulful. Under all that hair I had been hiding a pretty nice face—one with cheekbones and a dusting of freckles. The new short do was fringy and layered all over like a French starlet. I loved it.

Mom gasped when she saw me. "Oh, sweetheart. You are so gorgeous. Let me look at you." Natch, she started to cry. My mom the waterworks queen.

On the way to the car I kept catching sight of this new Lindsay in store windows. My head felt about three pounds lighter. I was walking taller and spunkier. You are your hair. A couple of grocery guys even checked me out. Judging from the blue-hair-and-dentures crowd that was shuffling out of the grocery store, I wasn't banking on that being a big thing—they were probably starved for girls under seventy. But still, it made me feel flirty.

The reporters had staked out the back way now, but Mom drove right through them. They did a double take, wondering who I was. It was sooo fun being mystery girl. I just wished Daniel were here to see my new look. Ha. Like he'd notice me after Suki.

Jeffrey met us on the side porch. If he was mad

at me for what I'd said to him last night, he wasn't acting like it. "Wow! Is this our Lindsay? Or is this some movie star who's come to our little wedding?"

It was the cheesiest of cheese lines. For the record, a cheesy line can be a beautiful thing. "Thanks," I said. I couldn't quite look him in the eyes. I needed to come clean before I was totally eaten up with guilt. "Mom? Do you mind if I have a few minutes with Jeffrey alone?"

Mom arched her famous eyebrow. "Hmmm, sounds very cryptic. Are you two plotting some devious surprise for later?"

Jeffrey laughed way too loud. I came to his rescue. "We could tell you, but then we'd have to kill you." It was such a Daniel line.

"All right," Mom said, breezing past us and leaving us with her yummy scent. "But this better not involve having to do the chicken dance later."

Jeffrey and I were alone. In the distance I could hear seagulls singing to each other. "I don't know how to say this, so I'm just going to throw it out there, okay? I am so, so sorry for the way I've been. It's like I was abducted by aliens and replaced with a pod person who was mean and surly and a bad sport. Plus she dressed funny."

Jeffrey cracked a smile and shook his head. "As the father of a complete fashion victim, I'm used to funny dressing."

"What I'm trying to say is, can we start over? No silly secrets. No cloak-and-dagger stuff. I just want you to make my mom happy. And I promise I'll stop acting like such a freak."

Jeffrey squeezed my shoulder and smiled. "I never thought I'd own a place like this. Never. You ever heard the phrase 'they didn't have a pot to piss in'?"

I nodded. "It means really poor, right?"

"It's about three steps below poor. That was us. I was kind of an angry kid. An orphan at a home. Got into a lot of trouble until I landed in front of Judge Leonard Bastrop. Lenny. He saw something in me, though I don't know what. And he gave me a second chance. Found a good home for me and made it possible for the stuff in my past to disappear. I made a promise to support him the way he supported me. Sometimes that was really hard, especially when he did something I found hard to accept. But a promise is a promise, and I honor my promises. I made mistakes, and he made mistakes."

I tried to imagine Jeffrey as this wild kid. It's always weird when you find out something about an adult that doesn't seem to fit who they are now. Like my mom and her Chief Yellowfeather stage. Or my dad, who was devoted to Miles, walking out on us when I was a baby. People had bends and twists in them just like roads and rivers. And just like roads and rivers, you never knew where they'd take you. You just had to hold on and go.

"Thanks for understanding," I said, slipping my hand into his.

Jeffrey gave my hand a warm, tight squeeze—

the squeeze of a man who knew how to hold on. "I'm not going anywhere, Lindsay. I promise you."

I knew he meant it. The sky was turning a soft baby blue, and the sun was riding high over the water. It was a perfect day for a wedding.

Fourteen

Daniel

IT WAS A gorgeous, sunny day at the beach with a babe I had been drooling about all summer. So why wasn't I having the time of my life? I needed to shake off the past twenty-four hours—the wild ride out here, that twister of a kiss with Lindsay, the big blow off followed by Lindsay burning rubber to get away. Weird stuff. As far as I was concerned, Lindsay and Sven could have that whole caviar scene. I was going to soak up a little local color, Suki style.

I was starving, and The Dock wasn't open yet, so Suki took me to a veggie-burger stand right off the beach. I wasn't usually wild about little green flecks in what should be a hard-core meat product, but I figured with enough ketchup and mustard, I could make anything edible. Suki ordered some kind of smoothie the color of tar. It smelled a little like tar too.

"What's that?" I asked through a mouthful of condiment-drenched veggie burger.

"It's a pinesap smoothie with wheat grass and alfalfa."

I laughed and choked down some sweet-potato chips that were a poor substitute for good old greasy Chee-tos. "It looks like something you'd clean off the bottom of your shoe."

I waited for a comeback, but Suki acted a little hurt. "Oh no. This is so great for your body. It really cleanses out all those toxins from fried foods and caffeine and sugar."

Okay. She'd just named the three corners of my food pyramid. I decided to try a different tack. "So, Suki. That's a different kind of name. Are your parents from California or something?"

"Michigan," she said without a single trace of irony. "I named myself. My birth name was Catherine." Score one for Hakeem.

"But you didn't dig Catherine? What, did people call you Cathy or Cat or some annoying nickname when you were in third grade and you vowed revenge?"

Suki took a big sip of her pinesap smoothie. "No. What do you mean?"

"Nothing," I said, munching on a chip. I really did not like sweet potatoes. "So you named yourself."

"Yeah. I had a whole rebirthing party with some friends last year and called myself Suki. It's, like, way more in tune with who I am."

"Oh." A rebirthing party? She hadn't really said that, had she? I pictured a bunch of tie-dye types lighting aromatherapy candles and telling Suki to come into the light. I finished the last of my mealy burger and threw the wadded-up, environmentally correct paper at the trash can. It bounced off the rim. Without a word Suki went over, picked it up, and put it in a different, blue trash can marked For Paper Only.

"Let's go for a walk on the beach." Suki laced her fingers through mine, and I felt this little electric jolt shoot straight to my heart and through the rest of my body like rush-hour traffic.

"Sure," I said. Now things were going somewhere.

We took off our shoes and let the warm sand scrunch up between our toes. I kind of wished the guys could see me like this, walking on the beach with a really hot chick like Suki. The conversation was a little awkward, though. Like we were different trains that couldn't get on the same track. It was not flowing. We got to a deserted spot near a pier, and Suki pulled me down on the sand. She started burying my feet in warm sand.

"So, tell me about this magazine you write for."

I totally didn't want to tell her it was a girls' magazine. "It's an online magazine. It's just a temporary gig for the summer. I'm looking into working for one of the big guys next summer. *Time. Newsweek.*"

"Oh," she said, biting her lip. She seemed

disappointed. "So are you, like, the music critic there?"

"No," I said. She was pouring sand over my legs. It probably should have been exciting, but it was making my calves itch. "I do features. Human interest. Profiles."

Suki's eyes sparkled, and she pushed me back in the sand to pour more wet, grainy stuff on my stomach. It was torture. "Really? Would you want to do a profile of me and my music?"

"Yeah," I said, totally distracted by something crawling up my shorts. "I could do that."

"Cool. 'Cause I think it would be so awesome if I could get some press. You know, it only takes one small break to make somebody."

I couldn't stand it. There was probably a bug the size of a Winnebago making a beeline for my butt. "Yeow!" I screamed, jumping up in a shower of flying sand. I hopped up and down like a maniac. Lindsay and I would have laughed out loud, and then she would have made some crack about how macho I was. Suki stared blankly like she'd seen guys hop up and down in the sand all day long. Maybe she had. I didn't know what was going on, but she was starting to annoy me. I still thought she was hot, but apparently I wasn't the only one. Suki seemed to be pretty big on Suki too. In fact, she hadn't asked me a single question about myself other than about the work I did for *Blink*.

"I think I've had enough of the beach," I said, sounding more irritated than I meant to let show.

Suki shrugged. "That's cool. Some friends of mine work at the ice stand in town. We could go hang there for a while."

I ordered up a triple mango ice while Suki introduced me to her friends, Kara and Nadine. A couple of guys Suki knew also stopped by. One of the guys was hitting on her big time. I chowed on my ice and watched this total tree-hugger dude hang all over Suki and tell her she was the next best thing to Jewel. I could tell Suki was totally eating it up. She kept finding reasons to touch the guy or lean past him for napkins or any of those stupid moves girls do to get close to guys without actually coming right out and saying so. A little free Guy's View advice for you? We are so on to you in the coy department, it's not even funny. Not that I want to discourage girls from leaning across me any chance they get.

Suki twirled a piece of hair and giggled while Tree Hugger practically thumped his chest caveman style. I wished Lindsay were here to make some smart-assed comment. The two of us would have a blast ripping on the whole scene. The sad fact was that Suki was a vain, social-climbing music weasel. She was looking for any guy who could put her face in *Spin* magazine. I wasn't that guy. I didn't want to be here. I wanted to be with Lindsay at Jeffrey's ugly estate, watching her mom get married while Alison gabbed on her cell phone and Marlon told the wedding guests they were bleeding brilliant. I wanted to put that big lug Sven on the next plane to Sweden. I wanted to hold Lindsay close and smell her clean neck while a band played a cheesy cover tune that we would make fun of later. And I wanted to kiss her again. And again. And again.

"What time is it?" I yelled, bolting out of my seat.

Suki looked perplexed. "Five o'clock," she said, taking note of the huge clock on the side of the ice stand. Duh.

"I gotta motor," I said.

Suki left the tree hugger so fast, it made me dizzy. She put her hand on my arm. "I thought you were gonna catch my gig, and then, you know, we'd hook up later."

"I wish I could," I said, checking my cash situation. Two quarters, a nickel, and some very old mints. Not good. I knew there was the emergency twenty-dollar bill in there that my dad told me to use in an emergency. I'd never used my dad's emergency money before. It was a point of pride with me. "I forgot that I have to write this article on the Forrester wedding, and I've already missed half of it. Anybody here wanna give me a ride?"

Five people stared at me. No one spoke. I pulled Suki aside and spoke in a hushed voice. I usually got quiet when I lied. "Listen, I shouldn't tell you this, but the Forresters own a couple of magazines. I'm pretty tight with his daughter. I think I might be able to help you out if you give me a ride."

Suki's greedy green eyes shone. Bingo. "My uncle is heading that way. I'll get him to give you a ride."

It was too ironic. I'd gotten into this whole mess because I wanted Lindsay to give me a ride to see Suki. Now I was begging Suki to give me a ride to see Lindsay. Life has a funny way of working out sometimes. All I had to do was grab my tux and . . . my tux. I hadn't realized until just now that I didn't have it. I was so excited about meeting up with Suki that I'd left it in the stables on the estate. If I lost that tux, my dad was out some serious moola, and I was going to be working it off till I was fifty.

Great. Now I had two reasons to hurry.

Lindsay

I felt pretty. I loved the new short do. I'd put on dangly pearl-drop earrings to celebrate the discovery of my neck and shoulders. And Mom had given Alison and me beautiful pearl chokers to wear. I also had to admit, as much as I didn't love pink, that the dresses were cool, like flapper dresses out of the twenties, complete with pearl-colored strappy sandals. I felt . . . grown up.

The "Wedding March" began, and everyone turned around to watch Mom practically float down the aisle in a formfitting ivory satin dress with little flowers beaded at the hem and sleeves. She wore her blond hair up high on her head like a princess. I stole a look at Jeffrey as she took his hand, and I could see that he was so in love with her, it hurt. I'd thought people only looked at each other that way in the movies, but Mom and Jeffrey were truly, hopelessly gaga over each other. This was what happiness looked like.

Everything was perfect: the flowers, the service, the music, the dresses, the feelings. There was only one thing missing. Sven took my hand to march me out during the recessional, and I closed my eyes for just a second, imagining that it was Daniel who was leading me back down the aisle toward the house for pictures. Maybe there was a happiness allotment. You could only have so much perfection in one day, and Mom and Jeffrey were entitled to it.

The pictures went by in a blur—all except for the one of Alison and me standing side by side. Why did I know that was the one that would end up on Mom's desk at work? Maybe I could sneak into her office someday and supply wicked little thought bubbles over our heads: "Stand any closer and I'll break your arm." "I can't get any closer—your ego keeps getting in the way." It's evil, but the evil thoughts get you through some bad spots.

It was nine o'clock before we made it out of the receiving line and into the reception for food. I was starving. I spied some amazing duck pizzas on a waiter's tray just as the bandleader made an announcement.

"Ladies and gentlemen, may I introduce to you Mr. and Mrs. Jeffrey Forrester." Mom and Jeffrey stepped onto the floor for their first dance together as husband and wife. Everyone stood.

The song ended, and a fast one began, which got everyone dancing. I wanted to avoid Sven, so I headed to the far end of the room and peered out the windows.

My breath caught in my throat. Daniel was running up toward the house, a goon three times his size on his trail.

I slipped out the door, trying to figure out how to save him.

"I wondered if you'd show up to claim your tux."

I whirled around. Jeffrey was behind me, smiling at Daniel. "He's a guest," Jeffrey whispered to the out-of-breath security guard.

Daniel stared at Jeffrey. Clearly neither of us knew what he was talking about.

"You left the tux in the stables," Jeffrey said. "It had the receipt with your name and address stapled to the outside."

"Oh," Daniel said.

"It's upstairs in my closet, near the front. I better get back. I've already warned your mom. It might have something do with her being a new bride, but she seemed pretty touched at all you two went through to be together at her wedding."

I felt like I might cry. I gave Jeffrey another kiss and a big hug. "You're the best. Thanks. And thank my mom, okay?"

Jeffrey nodded. His eyes seemed to be misty too.

Daniel cleared his throat. "Thanks, Mr. Forrester."

As Jeffrey walked away, I turned to face Daniel. He looked like he'd been through war. The expression on his face made my cheeks go all hot. I stared at the ground and kicked at the soft dirt with the point of my shoe. I wanted to ask about Suki, but I couldn't. "Go ahead. Make some crack about the froufrou dress."

"Wow," he said. And then softer, "Wow."

I felt funny. On display. I wanted him to say it again, and I wanted to run and hide behind a tree. Having the guy you adore give you props in the gorgeous department is a total roller-coaster ride. Suddenly I couldn't take it. I had to know. "So, what happened with Suki?"

"Funny thing. The whole time I was with her, I was thinking about you and how you're sort of the best thing that's happened to me in a long, long time. That was really hard to say, so I'd appreciate it if you could keep the sarcasm to a minimum, okay?"

I was smiling like an idiot, and I didn't care. "You moron. Don't you know I'm crazy about you?"

Daniel looked at me with those puppy-dog blue eyes. He started to say something, then smiled, embarrassed, and looked up at the sky like he was looking for one particular star. "Thanks," I heard him whisper.

"Who are you thanking?" I asked.

"No one," he said. He held out his hands to me. "Lindsay, may I have this dance?"

I stepped an inch closer. "Absolutely."

Fifteen

•

Daniel

LINDSAY AND I danced one perfect dance, and then, with Jeffrey's okay, I headed upstairs to shower and change. I can only admit this here, but taking a shower in a bathroom that's the size of a small apartment is so boss. Jeffrey's marble shower stall had enough gizmos to land planes at LaGuardia Airport. I tried five different water-massage settings and set the shower tunes (in stereo, no less) to my favorite alt-rock station. It was the best shower of my life.

I took extra-special care with the shaving. I wanted to look special for Lindsay. I kept seeing her, standing there on the lawn, all eyes and curvy mouth. Short hair was definitely a plus on her. This is gonna sound just one step up from a lite-FM song, but she really did look like a goddess—only in a Lindsay way, if that makes sense. It was like Lindsay to the tenth power. Or maybe I was finally able to see the real Lindsay. The point was, if I was going to cut it, I needed to put my tux and my mojo on. I hoped I was channeling my inner Cary Grant.

Lindsay was waiting for me at the bottom of the hall staircase, and when she saw me, I knew how it must feel to be the captain of the football team during a winning season.

"Wow, yourself," she said, putting her arms around me and giving me a nice, cozy squeeze.

"Hey. Watch the necktie. There's no way I can reproduce it if it goes awry."

A flash went off. Two photographers wearing *People* magazine passes were taking aim at us.

"I thought your mom was keeping these guys out."

"Are you kidding? My mom would die without at least one picture in a national publication. At least it's not the *Enquirer*."

The photographer flashed off another picture. "Hey, Lindsay. What's your friend's name?"

Lindsay's face went a little panicked. "Uh . . ."

"Daniel," I said. "Daniel Newman. I'm her boyfriend." My dad would just have to deal. If he didn't like rich people, well, I'd keep him off the social register. I grabbed Lindsay and dipped her in my arms in as suave a move as I could. Then I laid one on her. No lie—this was some kiss. Flashbulbs went off like bottle rockets. I'd say one thing, every time we kissed, there was some explosion going on. I pulled a shocked, smiling Lindsay back to her feet.

"Now they have a real picture," I said.

Epilogue

Daniel

Two weeks later . . .

"So," I SAID, stealing a french fry from Lindsay's plate at a diner near the *Blink* office. We sat on the same side of the booth. "When do your mom and Jeffrey get back from Italy?"

"This weekend. They called me last night. God, they sound so married. They even finish each other's sentences."

I smiled. "So, I'm just about finished with the profile on you and Alison. Want an advance copy?"

Lindsay grimaced. "I don't know. Do I?"

"Here, I'll read the best part to you. Oh, and there's a picture of us at the wedding, you in your princess dress and me in my Suki wear. The caption reads: 'Lindsay DeWitt is known both for her beauty and her sense of humor, as these pictures demonstrate.'"

She grinned and reached over and took a bite of my blintzes.

"I basically say that until you really know somebody, you don't know much about them at all, and that I learned that Alison Forrester and Lindsay DeWitt were both really interesting, complex people who cared about things other than shopping and gossiping."

Lindsay smiled and raised an eyebrow.

"Well, as an example, Alison is really into her cell phone."

Lindsay laughed. "You know, Alison and I spent a little time together these past couple of weeks. I doubt we'll ever be best friends, but I think we'll manage to be friends after a couple of years."

Like me and my dad. We'd made some headway these past couple of weeks ourselves. Letting each other be each other. That was really the key, I'd learned.

"So you and your dad are actually going to a Yankees game tonight?" Lindsay asked.

"Yup. Pretty cool. Bizarre thing—he wore a tie today. He did that last week too. I think he might be seeing somebody."

"Is that okay? Or does it freak you out?"

I thought about that. "A little of both. I guess it takes time getting used to new people in your life."

Lindsay nodded, and I took her hand and held it. At that moment I had never felt happier.

I pulled Lindsay into me and kissed her with everything I had. There were no firecrackers or flashbulbs this time. Just my heart beating a song—one that said everything was going to be fine. Better than fine.

The future was just beginning, and it had a name I couldn't stop hearing in every part of the city—in the steaming sidewalks and colorful, bustling crowds, in the stoops and doorways, in the neon lights over Times Square and the jagged-teeth-skyscraper skyline, in the walls of my room at night when I fell into a contented sleep, in my very soul. *Lindsay. Lindsay. Lindsay . . .*

Do you ever wonder about falling in love? About members of the opposite sex? Do you need a little friendly advice but have no one to turn to? Well, that's where we come in . . . Jenny and Jake. Send us those questions you're dying to ask, and we'll give you the straight scoop on life and love.

DEAR JAKE

Q: *The boy I like has no idea I'm alive. How can I get him to notice me?*

JC, New York, NY

A: How about . . . talking to him? Okay, I know it's not that easy, especially when you're supercrushing. Maybe you could find a reason to start a convo— something you have in common, perhaps. Talking to him is the best way to get him to notice you because he'll notice you for you. He'll notice how smart and funny or sweet or shy or wonderful you are. And that's how you want to get a guy's attention!

Q: *I'm what's referred to as a tomboy, and I'm great at sports.*

One of my friends told me guys aren't into that type of girl. Is she right?

AR, Plano, TX

A: Nope. Guys like all different types of girls, even if they think they have a "type." One of my girlfriends was a "girlie-girl" who wore makeup and high heels and perfume, and my next girlfriend was a tomboy like you who wore baseball caps, jeans, and sneakers every day. I don't think she ever wore a dress once! Be yourself, and trust me: You'll find a guy you like who likes you just fine the way you are.

DEAR JENNY

Q: *My boyfriend keeps telling me that he hates makeup and doesn't want me to wear any. But I think I look awful without makeup. What should I do?*

PK, Mesa, AZ

A: What makes *you* feel comfortable, what *you* like, and what makes *you* feel good about yourself: That's what counts. Still, tell the truth: If your boyfriend wore something every day that you didn't like, you sure would appreciate it if he didn't wear it—or at least not so often, right? So, perhaps a compromise is in order. You could wear less makeup than usual or forgo lipstick when you're with him.

Q: *I like a guy in my English class, but I can tell he likes the girl who sits in front of me. He's always staring at her. Should I just give up on my crush?*

BD, Edgewood, MD

A: Well, I guess you could give it a little time and see if they hook up. If they don't, that probably means he (a) didn't ask her out or (b) he did, and she said no. Either way, he's available! So maybe you should try a little harmless flirting and see how things go. Good luck!

Do you have any questions about love?
Although we can't respond individually to your letters,
you just might find your questions answered in our column.

Write to:
Jenny Burgess or Jake Korman
c/o 17th Street Productions,
an Alloy Online, Inc. company.
33 West 17th Street
New York, NY 10011

Don't miss any of the books in *Love Stories*
—the romantic series from Bantam Books!

#1 *My First Love* .... Callie West

#2 *Sharing Sam* .... Katherine Applegate

#3 *How to Kiss a Guy* .... Elizabeth Bernard

#4 *The Boy Next Door* .... Janet Quin-Harkin

#5 *The Day I Met Him* .... Catherine Clark

#6 *Love Changes Everything* .... ArLynn Presser

#7 *More Than a Friend* .... Elizabeth Winfrey

#8 *The Language of Love* .... Kate Emburg

#9 *My So-called Boyfriend* .... Elizabeth Winfrey

#10 *It Had to Be You* .... Stephanie Doyon

#11 *Some Girls Do* .... Dahlia Kosinski

#12 *Hot Summer Nights* .... Elizabeth Chandler

#13 *Who Do You Love?* .... Janet Quin-Harkin

#14 *Three-Guy Weekend* .... Alexis Page

#15 *Never Tell Ben* .... Diane Namm

#16 *Together Forever* .... Cameron Dokey

#17 *Up All Night* .... Karen Michaels

#18 *24/7* .... Amy S. Wilensky

#19 *It's a Prom Thing* .... Diane Schwemm

#20 *The Guy I Left Behind* .... Ali Brooke

#21 *He's Not What You Think* .... Randi Reisfeld

#22 *A Kiss Between Friends* .... Erin Haft

#23 *The Rumor About Julia* .... Stephanie Sinclair

#24 *Don't Say Good-bye* .... Diane Schwemm

#25 *Crushing on You* .... Wendy Loggia

#26 *Our Secret Love* .... Miranda Harry

#27 *Trust Me* .... Kieran Scott

#28 *He's the One* .... Nina Alexander

#29 *Kiss and Tell* .... Kieran Scott

#30 *Falling for Ryan* .... Julie Taylor

#31 *Hard to Resist* .... Wendy Loggia

#32 *At First Sight* .... Elizabeth Chandler

#33 *What We Did Last Summer* .... Elizabeth Craft

#34 *As I Am* .... Lynn Mason

#35 *I Do* .... Elizabeth Chandler

#36 *While You Were Gone* .... Kieran Scott

#37 *Stolen Kisses* .... Liesa Abrams

#38 *Torn Apart* .... Janet Quin-Harkin

#39 *Behind His Back* .... Diane Schwemm

#40 *Playing for Keeps* .... Nina Alexander

#41 *How Do I Tell?* .... Kieran Scott

#42 *His Other Girlfriend* .... Liesa Abrams

SUPER EDITIONS

Listen to My Heart . . . . Katherine Applegate
Kissing Caroline . . . . Cheryl Zach
It's Different for Guys . . . . Stephanie Leighton
My Best Friend's Girlfriend . . . . Wendy Loggia
Love Happens . . . . Elizabeth Chandler
Out of My League . . . . Everett Owens
A Song for Caitlin . . . . J.E. Bright
The "L" Word . . . . Lynn Mason
Summer Love . . . . Wendy Loggia
All That . . . . Lynn Mason
The Dance . . . . Craig Hillman, Kieran Scott, Elizabeth Skurnick
Andy & Andie . . . . Malle Vallik
Sweet Sixteen . . . . Allison Raine
Three Princes . . . . Lynn Mason

TRILOGIES

Max & Jane . . . . Elizabeth Craft
Justin & Nicole . . . . Elizabeth Craft
Jake & Christy . . . . Elizabeth Craft

Danny . . . . Zoe Zimmerman
Kevin . . . . Zoe Zimmerman
Johnny . . . . Zoe Zimmerman

London: Kit & Robin . . . . Rachel Hawthorne
Paris: Alex & Dana . . . . Rachel Hawthorne
Rome: Antonio & Carrie . . . . Rachel Hawthorne

LOVE STORIES: HIS. HERS. THEIRS.

#1 The Nine-hour Date . . . . Emma Henry

Coming soon:

#2 Snag Him! . . . . Gretchen Greene

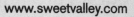

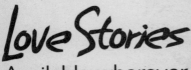